GETTING OVER
TOM

STORIES BY
ABIGAIL THOMAS

SCRIBNER PAPERBACK FICTION
Published by Simon & Schuster
New York London Toronto Sydney Tokyo Singapore

SCRIBNER PAPERBACK FICTION
Simon & Schuster Inc.
Rockefeller Center
1230 Avenue of the Americas
New York, NY 10020

First Scribner Paperback Fiction Edition 1995
Published by arrangement with Algonquin Books of Chapel Hill

SCRIBNER PAPERBACK FICTION and design are trademarks of Simon & Schuster Inc.

Manufactured in the United States of America

1 3 5 7 9 10 8 6 4 2

Grateful acknowledgment is made to *Columbia—A Magazine of Poetry and Prose, Glimmer Train, The Little Magazine, Missouri Review,* and *The Santa Monica Review,* where some of the stories first appeared.

Grateful acknowledgment is made for permission to quote from "Dixie Chicken" © 1972, by Lowell George and Martin Kibble, published by Naked Snake Music.

Library of Congress Cataloging-in-Publication Data
Thomas, Abigail.
    Getting over Tom : stories / by Abigail Thomas.
        p.   cm.
    1. Man-woman relationships—United States—Fiction.   2. Women
—United States—Sexual behavior—Fiction.   3. Sexual addicts—
United States—Fiction.   I. Title.
[PS3570.H53G47   1995]
813'.54—dc20   95-21075
                                                          CIP

ISBN 1-56512-024-8
       0-684-81347-5 (pbk.)

Thanks to my kids, the best in the world: Sarah, Jennifer, Ralph, and Catherine. Thanks to my dear sister, Eliza. Thanks to old pals Chuck Verrill, Liz Darhansoff, Quin Luttinger. Thanks to Shannon Ravenel, my editor. Thanks to my parents for teaching me to notice. And thanks to Rich, my husband, for just about everything.

For my family

CONTENTS

GETTING OVER TOM

GETTING OVER NOW

"You don't glide into love. You fall."
—*C. T. Verrill*

PART ONE

SISTERS

Once again our mother is disabled by love. Carmine is back. Carmine, who came before Henry Gold and then vanished, has reappeared now, after Henry and toward the end of Martin. Henry was a poet, Martin burned his house down, and Carmine is a guido from Yonkers. Big white car, red upholstery. The usual bad boy. My mother likes the bad boys. It isn't seemly. Plus, she is old enough to be his mother.

"Stepmother," she corrects me. "Don't say 'guido,'" she scolds, narrowing her eyes, as if this had any effect on me. She has been watching *Woodstock* the movie tonight and it made her cry, probably because she didn't get to go. The closest she came was that our baby-sitter went. "There's Alice!" she said, getting excited, pointing to a naked girl in a pickup who was on the screen for one instant. I

3

remember Alice. She used to blow reefer in our faces when we went to the playground. I tell my mother this now.

"She did what?" I have my mother's full attention. A novelty.

"All the time," horns in Janet. "We *loved* it."

"Jesus Christ," says our mother. "Thank God I didn't know that then." And she turns back to the movie.

"What were you doing?" I ask, just to keep her talking.

"In 1968?" My mother squints up at the ceiling briefly. "Banging the boss, probably," she replies. This is a typically inappropriate bit of information, given that I am thirteen and Janet will be ten tomorrow. Then she gets to her feet and leaves the room. She is always leaving the room to do something important somewhere else. A foot out every door. The woman is double-parked through life.

"What's 'banging'?" Janet asks me. I cannot believe that she does not know the facts of life, so I fill her in but she thinks I'm kidding. "You're crazy," she says. "Nobody would *do* that."

"*Au contraire*," I say, with some satisfaction. We hate each other's guts. "Your mother is doing it *constamment*."

So Janet gives me a rabbit punch, which is no inconsiderable blow given that she possesses the killer instinct. She also lifts weights. Coffee cans filled with rocks, rocks from my rock collection, too, another sore point. "Why can't you go out and get your own rocks?" I have asked her. "Why does it have to be my good rocks?"

"You call common quartz a good rock?" She will answer. "Shale? Limestone? Cement?" This is one of Janet's most annoying qualities—she knows more than I do about the things I love.

Tonight we have a knock-down-drag-out fight, and she pulls out a big clump of hair over my left ear so that I will have to wear a barrette for weeks, and does our mother care? I believe that with strength should come responsibility, I believe our mother should yell at Janet, but when I come crashing into the kitchen bald as a bat, all she says is, "Don't show me anything," in that ominous voice. She is stirring something at the stove and refuses to turn around. Then Janet pipes up, "Stephanie spit on me," and I see our mother's body go stiff as an ironing board and then she throws a spatula clear across the kitchen into the sink.

"Jesus Christ! If you think I have the slightest interest

in spending the rest of my life looking at who spat where first," she is practically screaming, "you are sadly mistaken!" Then she stomps out of the kitchen and we hear her bedroom door slam. Very adult behavior, and this is my role model. I guess Carmine hasn't called.

"Brilliant, you little slime," I say to Janet. "You couldn't see what kind of mood she was in?"

"You started it."

I could kill Janet. I really could. Sometimes I look at her big white forehead and her teeth and her little eyebrows and I could just kill her. If I had a button I would push it. Once she did almost die. She fell out of the car when we were little. It was night, and our mother was driving with the radio on loud to keep herself awake, and I had to call "Mom" several times from the back seat before she heard me. "Mother," I finally yelled, "Janet isn't in the car anymore." When we found her, she was sitting up in the middle of the road, completely unhurt. Janet is made out of rubber. I wish I had kept my mouth shut. I wish we had just left her there.

I don't really remember that, I've just heard our mother tell the story. It is usually Janet who remembers things. Where I can remember a vague shape, she can tell me how many windows. If I recall the pear tree, she can come up with the sundial, the kind of pears, and the pear picker, which she says I lost. It is annoying, because she acts as if the past belongs to her just because she remembers it better, as if I hadn't been there at all.

The thing is, I am fairly sure that I was once alive in Egypt. Certain shades of blue have always given me a funny feeling, as well as certain shapes of bugs, and I recognize them now to be the colors and scarabs familiar to ancient Egyptians. This might be why my memory is bad, it has to stretch back so far. Janet is a newer soul, she remembers things of this life better. Our mother is a brand-new soul, and it is tough to have a beginner for a mother. How else to explain her behavior? She will stand up in the kitchen making kissing noises with Carmine even if I am sitting right there eating my snack.

I specialize in the present and the future. I know for certain that our mother has forgotten that tomorrow is Janet's tenth birthday. I do not plan to remind her, I am not nice enough, but I do try to prepare Janet for her disappointment. "Wise up," I say, "she's got her mind on the Italian stallion. *Amo, amas, amat.* Don't take it personally." We are in our room. Janet is lying on the floor drawing a horse.

"She hid the presents. She's planning to surprise me." Janet says this without looking up. She is drawing the nostrils and the lips now, her favorite part. I like to watch her put the little whiskers in the chin, but I don't let her know this. She is wearing the smile she has when she's getting ready to cream me in checkers or get some damn triple word score using her *z*. This is when I hate her the most.

But I'm right, of course. The next morning at breakfast there is no mention of birthday, which only serves to confirm Janet's surprise party theory. I feel a little sorry for her. Our mother hurries us off to school. Apparently Carmine called late last night. His father is sick, and our mother wants to rush to his, Carmine's, side. "Isn't his own mother there?" I ask, but under my breath. My mother throws me a dirty look, but she doesn't ask me to repeat what I said. She is thirty-two years old. Carmine is twenty-three. I like Carmine. He used to bring us coffee cake and hand-packed ice cream. Once he drove us to Virginia for a vacation. He didn't have a job then, and he lived with us for a couple of months and we would come home and find he had painted the living room red, or the bathroom purple, or our room pumpkin colored. Our mother made us say we loved it. "We don't want to hurt his feelings," she would say.

When we get home from school our mother is gone, she has had the nerve to leave us a note saying Carmine's father has died and she wants us to call Carmine and tell him how sorry we are. How sorry we are? Instead of how pleased and delighted that Carmine's father, Sal, has finally bitten the dust and now Carmine can keep the car? I jest. It's just that I hate being told to do what I would ordinarily want to do on my own.

As for our own father, where is he? Utica? Buffalo? Geneseo? Who knows? He sang us songs. He sang us "Foggy Foggy Dew." He sang us "Dinah Won't You Blow." He sang us "Swing Low, Sweet Chariot." But he slept every day until five o'clock and then he demanded breakfast. Eggs over easy. Scrambled dry. Our mother threw custard cups at him and he slapped her. "Enough of this shit," she said one day, and we all got on the airplane except him. Outside the plane was thunder and lightning and we were on our way forever, not just the summer. We expected our father to come after us and drag us home, but he never did. We used to hide under the covers night after night, waiting for him. I never discuss him with

Janet. She will remember something I don't and another piece of him will belong to her.

Tonight Janet is pretending she doesn't care about her birthday, and I tell her that Carmine being back means Italian Thanksgiving again. She hates red food. I am just trying to distract her. We cook two TV dinners, and I let her have the turkey with stuffing, which is our favorite, and I eat the horrible Salisbury steak. Then we mix up a box of Duncan Hines yellow cake and we take it in the bathroom and sit on the edge of the tub and eat the whole thing without cooking it, which makes us almost puke. Then I give her a pack of Newports I filched from our mother's bag. It only takes her three tries to get one lit. She's a fast learner.

Then we play a game of checkers. Usually I hate the way she puts her men down so softly, I like to hear a clink on the board. But I am thinking about the pear tree, I am remembering how it hung out over a curve in the road, dropping pears until the road was slippery and sweet, and how the yellow jackets hung around. If I say this now, she will tell me how many yellow jackets and where their nest was, and how they stung her and her face swelled up like a melon. Whenever Janet gets hurt she compares it to

some form of food. But finally I ask her if she remembers
the time I fell out of the pear tree and broke my wrist and
our father carried me home in his arms.

"He took me to the emergency room," is all she says,
"the night I had a fit. He carried me the whole way in
just his bathrobe." I don't say anything. "King me," she
whispers.

At ten-thirty there is still no sign of our mother, and we
decide to teach her a lesson by pretending we have been
murdered. I forget whose idea this is, but we strew our
clothes in a scary trail from the front door to the bathroom,
underpants, undershirts, socks, all our white clothes, like
big bread crumbs. Then we get the broom and a lot of
blankets and we get into the tub with the light off. Janet
sticks the broom upside down between her arm and her
side, which looks in the gloomy light as if the broom is
sticking right out of her heart. I just get my body in a
funny position, like a pretzel. Janet falls asleep first and
the broom sags, and I just lie there and listen to her
breathe. Usually I hate the little sighs she makes in her
sleep, as if she is trying to get attention for being so cute,
but tonight I do not. Tonight I almost like her. I have
heard your true soul shows when you are asleep and I

never let anyone see me with my eyes closed. I am afraid I have a ratty soul. But Janet looks all right, she looks sort of blank, like a piece of paper.

Next thing I know we are getting waked up by our mother snapping the light on, rattling the shower curtain back. The broom is fallen over. "What's going on here?" she wants to know and she bends down. She is wearing lipstick and powder, and her face smells good. I am blinking in the light, but I can see Carmine behind her in the doorway, his arms full of presents. I have nothing against Carmine, he looks nice and serious, it is my mother who drives me crazy, how she acts around men. "Here precious," she says, and gives me a kiss, which I wipe off, and a bag of amaretto cookies, which are the kind that cut your mouth to pieces unless you dip them in coffee, which she knows I hate, and to Janet she gives a bag of disgusting marzipan. "Both of you say thank you to Carmine," she says, and then she reaches for Janet, who is smiling her head off and climbing out of the tub into our mother's arms like a baby, and I am back to hating her again and everyone, all of them smiling as if they are so happy, as if everything is going to be all right.

SEEING THINGS

It is the terrible summer we all go crazy. Uncle Peach has offed himself and I now sleep in my clothes. Maybe we hardly knew him, but his blood runs in our veins. There is lunacy in this family, and I feel too peculiar in my floaty nightgown. I know I am a child, but I am a tall child, and children can go crazy too. Look at Lizzie Borden. "Lizzie Borden was an adult," my mother informs me, her words hard to make out with the toothbrush in her mouth. She spits into the sink. We are nearing the moment I dread the most. In a matter of minutes she will by lying in her bed, fast asleep, utterly helpless. At the mercy of someone who might be a complete maniac. It is not normal to fear sleepwalking. It is not normal to think I will rise in the night and stab my mother to death with the barbecue fork.

"Relax," says my mother, without a backward glance. "I'll hear you coming."

This is not reassuring. My mother is not a dumbbell, but nurture is not her middle name. When I grow up, I plan to hit the road. I will travel the world, and live by my wits, and never have any children of my own. I can hardly wait. Meanwhile, I am stuck here with my mother and my sister Maude.

I never feel like killing Maude, thank goodness, I don't know why. She is my older sister, nearly fifteen. I climb into bed with Maude when mother's light goes out. Maude protects me with her normal wholesome snores. Her great ambition is to be whistled at on the street. Above her bed, taped to the ceiling, is her poster of Hawaii, Hawaii from the Air. She likes to lie on her back and pretend she is coming in for a landing. She plans to live in Hawaii some day. Poor Maude. She will be surrounded by nincompoops in flowered shirts. She will find pineapple in all her food. She does not care. Maude wants to be tan the whole year round. She wants to wear a hula skirt and do the hula dance. "Hubba hubba, ding dong," says Maude. I myself will visit the medieval cities of Europe. Kracõw. Dubrovnik, Prague. I am a more serious person and was born with a melancholy soul.

Maude is sick in bed and bored to death. Last Tuesday she came into the kitchen wearing only her slip. "Look at this interesting bone," she said, and pointed to her shoulder. My mother dropped the plates she was carrying and they smashed to the floor. You could see Maude's bones sticking out all over the place. You could see her ribs from the back. She looked like a skeleton. "Jesus Christ," shrieked our mother, as if this were all Maude's fault, "what are you doing to yourself, Maude? Jesus fucking Christ!" Mother's face had gone all pink and then all white.

"Don't say 'fucking'!" I screamed at her, and pretty soon Maude was crying and yelling, "There's nothing wrong with me, I'm sorry I even mentioned it!" But none of us could move, we were all barefoot and the broken plates were on the floor, and we could only lean toward each other screaming from our fixed positions. It was almost funny. Finally I instructed Mother and Maude to climb up on chairs, and I managed to clear a path with wet paper towels. I am the one who perfected this technique, although you can never get it all up, we will be stepping on glass forever from time to time.

It turns out Maude has chicken pox, which is very embarrassing for Maude. The doctor said she should sleep in the back room where it's quiet. She wants me to bring her lipstick and mirror from the *salle de bain*. "You look fine," I say.

"You lie like a rug," says Maude. She has a cute doctor and she wants to look her best morning noon and night in spite of everything. "Bring me the Erace," Maude commands.

"You've got to be kidding," I say.

She does not appreciate that I keep finding constellations on her arm and back. "The Big Dipper," I say, to try and get her mind off herself. "Really, they are just like little stars," I go on, but Maude groans.

"Go away," she says. "Go away. Get me something to drink," she says, without adding a please. When I come back with cold lemonade she doesn't want it. "Not that," she says. "Not that. I don't know what. Water."

Maude is getting a lot of attention.

The first night she is in the other room I try and stay up as long as I can. I lie on her bed and stare at Hawaii. When Mother's light goes out I have these terrible fears that something will come out from under the bed, or behind the curtain, some terrible monster that will be me. So I snap my light on. I think of all the names of all the different kinds of cat. I recite the alphabet backward in under one minute. I do the Lord's Prayer with feeling. "Deliver us from evil," I say this part over and over. I get out of bed and brush my hair one hundred strokes. I gargle with salt. When I see my mother's light go on I run quickly back into bed and close my eyes. I hear her tiptoe in and turn my light out and tiptoe out again. Sometimes I feel sorry for her. She is so easy to fool. But miracle of miracles I fall asleep and wake up without having killed anyone.

Peach killed himself, but not in the normal way. He did not drive his car off a bridge or eat pills or blow his brains out. Instead, Peach shot off both his ears while he was sitting in his rowboat, and then he drifted around and got tangled up in some low-hanging trees in a bushy part of the lake. Nobody really knows what happened, and it makes you want to laugh, which is so terrible, because it wasn't funny at all.

My mother won't discuss it. I asked her what happened to his body. "Where is he buried?" I wanted to know.

"Please," said my mother in one of her final tones of voice. "Please. Don't ask."

We only knew him that one summer. He had wandered

around his whole life and come to settle down at Lake Monroe, in a cabin he built all by himself. He had gypsy feet, he told us, but now they'd found a home. We went up last summer and drank the lake water, which was green in our glass, and our mother made coffee out of it and she and Peach leaned against the tree trunks while Maude and I went fishing. There was no running water and no electricity and no clocks. I rode around on Peach's shoulders, and he called me his special girl because he said I would turn out tall, like him. He was so handsome he could catch bees in his bare hands.

But he heard things. What things? "A kind of ringing," said Peach, "that goes on and on." Voices, too. What did they say? Peach never told us. Maybe they were evil voices. Maybe they told him what to do.

I see things, that is all, but they are not people, and they never speak to me. They are shapes, mostly, and they hurry along the wall and disappear into the cracks of the ceiling. I see them out the corners of my eyes. "Floaters," says my mother, who is not concerned. Bits of debris on the surface of my eyeball. "Quite common," she tells me. I don't take my mother's word for it. I close my eyes and try to imagine tiny little pieces of driftwood bobbing around under my lids, but it's impossible. What I see looks real.

My mother is nearsighted. She sees things, too. Once she thought she saw a goose being walked down Broadway. "My God!" she practically shouted. "A goose!"

"That is a cat, mother dear," I informed her. A white cat with its tail in the air. I have twenty-twenty vision. Another time she thought she saw a lady's camisole drifting by our living room window, but it was just a plastic Baggie from nowhere. "I prefer it my way," my mother says, in a snooty voice.

Maude gets very jealous. She never sees anything. She cannot stand it that I do, that I am more interesting than she is. So she pretends, just to get my goat.

"Did you notice her?" Maude will tease me.

"Who?"

"The woman in the red coat. She just walked through the wall. First she sat on your bed, though. She had a little dog with her. He licked my hand. A Jack Russell terrier, I believe." Maude will go through this performance just to annoy me. She has a fertile imagination when she cares to use it, but she has not had ghosts for visitors. For instance, the spot on the bed was neither cold nor warm. Ghosts are never just room temperature.

Maude is cranky beyond belief.

"I detest staying in bed," says Maude. "Do you have any idea how tedious my life has become?"

I shake my head.

"And how revolting it is to have chicken pox at my age?" she continues. "Absolutely revolting. Why can't it be mono? Why can't it be something romantic?"

I shake my head again.

"The only consolation I have is that you will get them next," says Maude.

"Stop scratching," I tell her. She is wearing little white gloves from our dead grandmother.

"I'm only scratching where it doesn't show," she says.

If you sit still in this room the traffic noises come through in a kind of crashing hum. It reminds me of the ocean which reminds me of the lake which reminds me of Uncle Peach. Why did he do what he did? Sometimes I think if I could figure out the answer I would know everything in the world I need to know. But there is no answer. That's what Maude says. How can you find a reason for an irrational act? is what Maude says. "Besides," she likes to speculate, "maybe it was all just a big accident. Maybe he shot one ear by mistake and then the other to remain symmetrical." This story illustrates the basic difference between me and Maude: She does not take one thing seriously.

Tonight our mother is sitting in the living room with the telephone on her lap. She is dialing information for one city after another, looking for Dad. We must be very low of funds. This only happens when we are about broke. Dad left seven years ago. He needed his space. He gave our mother three thousand dollars and a gold watch, which she instantly pawned. I look at her and see that her face has assumed the pointy look it gets when she is worried. She glances at me.

"Make a suggestion," she says.

"Biloxi?" I like the sound of the name. "Chattanooga?"

These cities annoy her and she lights another cigarette. In vain have I told her of the danger to all who live beneath her smoky roof. Mother does not do well under trying conditions. The condition of being somebody's mother. But I can see how upset she is, and I attempt a few words of comfort. This is my nature.

"Don't worry," I tell her. I even touch her shoulder. "Everything will be okay." I say this out of the goodness of my heart, not from any conviction. She does not smile at me or pat my hand. She does not say thank you, or it will or it won't. Silly me. This would be entirely out of character, although a little reassurance might be nice when your sister is languishing with a childhood disease and your mother has gone crazy on the couch. Instead, she gets up and goes into the bathroom. I can hear her crying two minutes later, even though she turns the water on full blast. Alas, I can do nothing. We do not get along.

I wash her teacup and yell to her is she hungry but receive no reply, so I heat up a can of ravioli and finish the whole thing myself. Then I turn on a program about tigers, which shows the actual eating of one live animal by another. I find this quite shocking and watch it with the sound turned off. It's not as bad without the crunching. Then I fall asleep on the couch. Later I get waked up by the Mexicans who live across the street. Or Guatemalans, I don't know. They take up the whole fourth floor of the hotel, and they play their saddest songs late at night when regular people are sleeping. I cannot keep a North American dream wrapped around their cries. Then I hear

Maude calling for a glass of juice. Our mother sleeps with three pillows over her head so she is useless at night, as well as a sitting duck. I get Maude something to drink, and then I lie down at the foot of her bed on the floor like a dog. I feel safer in here.

I dream I am flying, me and Maude, who is in the dream, too. Not exactly flying, more like taking these enormous hops. Peach is in there, too, and the closer we hop, the farther back he melts. "It isn't flying that's difficult," Maude tells me in our dream. We are suddenly standing on the roof looking down at the street. "It's landing." If I tell her this, Maude will take credit for the wisdom even though she said it in my head, in my dream.

In the morning after our mother goes to work, I hunt for money. Maude wants cigarettes and we are out of milk. I am standing in my mother's closet going through her pockets when I hear the front door open and close. Jesus Christ, Mother back for something and me in her sacred closet going through her sacred pockets for a little sacred loose change. So I step back and dislodge something from the shelf where she keeps her winter boots. A can of something. Heavy. Mother hollers good-bye again, and I hear the front door bang behind her and I bend down and look. It is not a can of paint. It is Peach. Ashes of Peach. Peach Ribley, it says on the label. So I sit right down on the floor of the closet on top of all the shoes.

The can is cool. It weighs maybe five pounds. I hold it up to my ear, but there is no sound whatsoever. Only me breathing in my mother's closet and the smell of shoes. I wonder how six feet three of somebody could be boiled down so small. "Peach," I whisper, "why were you so nice?" But I get no answer. "Peach," I say a few more times. "Uncle Peach."

IT IS a beautiful day and I have Peach in a shopping bag with flowers all over it. I have a can opener in my pocket. Down by Seventy-ninth Street you can stand next to the river with only a low fence. First I sit down on a bench and punch holes in the top of the can. This is to free his spirit, and also so he can float out into the water. I can't open the whole can and let the ashes drift down, because it is too windy and also somebody might see. Then I try to think of some words to say, but I can't, only his name. "Here darling Peach," I say and throw the can as far as I am able into the water. The river leads to the ocean and the ocean leads everywhere. I hope I did the right thing.

There's no undoing it. All the way home I see bodies. I see newspaper bodies, tangled garbage bodies, shadow bodies. Twisted thrown-out-old-clothes bodies. Maybe this means I will see dead bodies all over the place for the rest of my life.

I go straight to Maude. I want to tell her what I have done. I want her to say something that will make me laugh, or tell me something she did that was worse, which is what she is good for. Or just put me in my place. "For God's sake," I want her to say. "You're just a little kid. What do you expect?" But Maude is in a bad mood. All she wants to talk about are cigarettes. "I can't give you a cigarette," I tell her. "You look ridiculous smoking with the chicken pox," I tell her, but in this regard Maude is as single-minded as our mother. Jesus Christ. So I go find her a cigarette, and Maude smokes it and then she falls asleep.

So I just sit around on the chair. I am remembering something Peach told us once. He knew about a lake where all the dragonflies in the world are born and every year at the end of summer they come flying back from everywhere to touch the surface of the lake once more before they die. Peach cried when he told us that. I felt so bad, but I didn't know what to say. I wish I had said something. I wish I hadn't of just sat there like a moron staring at the water.

"You aren't paying any attention to me," says Maude. Her voice startles me.

"You were asleep," I tell her. "You were fast asleep."

"I was not. I never sleep in here. I just close my eyes."

"How are you feeling?" I ask cautiously.

"I feel a little better," she says. "Actually."

"The Big Dipper is fading," I say, for a joke, but she doesn't crack a smile.

"Seen anything recently?" she asks me. An odd question, coming from Maude.

"Nothing that wasn't there," I say. An odd answer, coming from me.

Maude is quiet. She looks as if she is deciding whether to tell me something or not.

"I think I did."

"What?"

"Or else I had a very vivid dream."

"What?" I say. "What?"

"Peach," says Maude. "Sort of hovering over my bed. Did you see him? A minute ago?"

"Missed it," I say. I feel very warm all of a sudden.

"Honest to God," says Maude. "I am not fooling. He was dressed like an angel, wings and everything. He said the word "accident," and he looked over at you. He seemed fine. He didn't look miserable, and there wasn't any blood. He was wearing earmuffs."

"Earmuffs?"

"Now do you believe me?"

"Nope," I say. I look down at her serious face. "I don't know, Maude. Why should I?"

"He said you would want proof. He told me to give you this," and Maude opens her hand, but there is nothing in it.

"What?" I say. "He told you to give me what?"

"He took a feather out of one of his wings. I know it's here someplace," says Maude. "Help me find it, will you? He left not three minutes ago. He just sort of disintegrated into thin air."

"Three minutes angel time," I say to her kindly. "Angels have a whole different way of keeping time from us." But I poke around on her bed, because I feel sorry for her. I wonder if she has got a fever and I touch her forehead, which is cool as a cucumber. Then I find a longish odd-looking feather among the bedclothes, which is no doubt from her pillow. "That's it!" says Maude, triumphant. "That's it! It's for you! He said so."

"What color earmuffs?" I ask her, holding the feather up to the light. Weird feather.

She shuts her eyes. "Blue, I think," she says. "Yes, blue." And then, like a light bulb, Maude is asleep.

I KEEP the feather in my bottom drawer. It is quite long, longer than your average pillow feather. It is not soft like a plume, and nothing like a quill. It is nothing like anything, to tell the truth. And Maude has forgotten the entire incident. She has no memory of having seen Peach at all, or of the feather. So it's sort of as though he appeared only to me, and in the kindest way possible. Like in a mirror. He must have known that if I saw him directly it would affect my brain. I would totally freak. I would have to think I might be crazy. So he appeared to Maude, to soften the blow. And it must have been an accident after all. Just a terrible accident. Maude was right all along.

TONIGHT MY mother is reading in the living room.

"I saw something today," I tell her, making it up as I go along. "A body. Right in the middle of the street." I pause, to see if she is interested in this story. She lowers her book. Maybe she understands I am giving her a rare opportunity to show concern. Out of the goodness of my heart. "It looked like a run-over angel, and I was the only person around."

"An angel?" she asks.

I nod my head.

"What kind of angel?" she asks.

"How many kinds are there?" I say. "It was an angel angel. A good angel. Big white wings, feathers. The works. Run over right in the middle of the street." I feel like crying all of a sudden, even though it isn't true.

"Oh dear," says my mother, "what a sad sight." This is such an unexpected answer that I don't know what to say next. "What did you do?" she asks after a moment. "I hope you didn't go charging out into traffic." And she knits her brow, just like a real mother.

"It wasn't an angel when I got up close," I tell her. "It was more like a bunch of old clothes."

"A bunch of old clothes," repeats my mother. "Well." She studies my face. "You can't kill an angel, anyway," she says. She sounds so positive, but she always sounds most positive when she doesn't know what she's talking about.

"You think?" I ask.

"I'm sure," she says. "You were probably right the first time. It probably was an angel. He's probably flying around all over the place right now." She looks so serious I have to smile.

"Mother," I say, "get a grip."

"There's more to life than meets the eye," says my mother, and she picks up her book again. The rug is littered with balled-up pieces of paper. My mother is reading *Love Story*, and every time she finishes a page she rips it out and crumples it up and throws it on the floor. "It's trash," she explains. "This is the only sane response."

In the middle of the night I get waked up by the Mexicans again. They are out on the roof, singing one of their yipping songs. Mother says they are homesick, and that it's sad they come a long way to freeze in a doorway somewhere. Maude says she sees them every morning with their baskets of gladiolas to sell, and they look fine to her. I don't know what to think. If I look down at them in the morning I can see the little pink dots of scalp on top of their heads. They are dancing like crazy over there. They look like children from above.

1957

Loretta and I are locked in the upstairs bathroom with her mother's makeup spread out on the sink. I am wearing it all: rouge, powder, eyeliner, the works. Perfume, too. "Just a dab on your pulse points," my mother says, but I say just upend the bottle and pour a couple of slugs down your shirt. Which I do. Now we are lighting matches, practicing for the rainy day when we have only soggy matchbooks. We try our asses, our kneecaps, the zippers of our jeans as we've seen Benny Soutar do. Zippers work best.

Loretta dries her teeth with a washcloth; she is getting ready to strike a match on the two big ones in front. "You're degenerating," I tell her. I have the most makeup on. Loretta has two clown spots on her cheeks and some pink on her lips. Loretta has lips like a rubber band.

"Now you're just playing with matches like a baby, Loretta," I tell her.

"I am not playing with matches. I am preparing for each and every emergency. And I am perfecting my cool."

"There is nothing cool about lighting a match on your teeth," I tell her. I am in a bad mood. Loretta is my best friend, but I know I'm going to need a new one soon.

"It is cool to know how and then resist," she says, which is too dumb to even answer.

"All right," I say. "One hand." I take the matchbook in my right hand and bend a match over double to the striking part and rub it with my thumb the way I have seen Benny do, but it catches the whole thing on fire and I have to drop it and step on the little flaming wad. The floor is pink and black tile like everything else in this damn bathroom. Even the shower curtain is pink with little black dolphins on the hem.

"Shit," I say.

"On a stick," says Loretta. She can swear without using a single four-letter word. It is one of her art forms.

Now we are smoking. I am showing her how to french inhale. I've got an L & M going and she has a Parliament, and we're looking sideways in the mirror to get the sexy angle, and I'm just about doing it when Loretta says, "Seems kind of pointless, doesn't it?" which cracks me up, but then I get mad because I've lost the knack. Loretta fills up her cheeks with smoke and makes a little pursey fish mouth and taps her cheek very gently and out come a million tiny smoke rings, one after another, like a stream of bubbles. "Oh, that's very sexy," I tell her. She doesn't look at me, just keeps tapping.

This girl does not get it. School starts tomorrow. She just does not know what we're up against.

So now we're downstairs, and we're about to have a best friends ceremony like last year. We're too old for this, but we're doing it anyway. We're going to write our names on two pieces of paper and cut them in the shape of a heart, and then we fold up the heart into a tiny ball and I swallow Loretta's name and she swallows mine. But before I'm done cutting mine, she takes her yo-yo and starts to walk-the-dog. It is annoying and I say, "Oh, Loretta, grow up." Then she bats the paper with her yo-yo, which is more annoying than I can say. Loretta is skillful with a yo-yo. If there were Yo-yo Olympics, Loretta would win the gold.

"Grow up? You mean like you, Miss Sexual Universe?" she says, and she rolls her heart into a spitball and flicks it at me. I hold mine up and start to tear it in half very slowly and deliberately, and she aims her yo-yo at it again, which makes me take out my lighter and set the whole thing on fire, and she slaps it with her hand and the burning piece falls on the rug. Well, something must have spilled on the shag that burns fast, because we first try to stomp it, and then Loretta yells for me to get the kettle, and she grabs the blanket off the couch and runs to the bathroom. "*Loretta, get back here this minute!*" I am running in a circle around the edges pouring this thin wobbly stream of water, and the room is getting smoky with those little black floaters in the air, and Loretta comes charging back with a wet blanket and we manage to lay it on the rug, which does the trick. Good thing her mother is at work.

We just stand there a minute, and then Loretta goes to open the window and says, "I think you better go home now," with her back to me. And I do.

Loretta and I stay mad for two days, which is the longest we've ever gone without speaking. Then I break down and tell her she is invited to Marcie Nevers's party on Saturday. I am too nice to tell her this was my doing. People are starting to like me. Particularly Benny Soutar, who is in the eleventh grade. Marcie knows if I come then Benny will come; if Benny comes, Jimmy Danvers comes, and Eddie, and the rest of it. I have never had so much power. Right away I said, "How about Loretta?" and Marcie shrugged. "Does that mean yes?" I asked.

"Okay," said Marcie. "If she has to."

"A SPIDER spins alone," says Loretta when I tell her. Spider is her nickname, Loretta Spider Wilson. She is up in the tree over Etra Road, and she's got her four yo-yos going, two hands and two feet, she's walking the dog like mad. Loretta cuts out rubber gloves to fit over her toes so she won't get blisters. She can do all the tricks: shoot-the-moon, loop-the-loop, milk-the-cow, round-the-world, but walking-the-dog is her favorite, and she swings her gangly self up in the tree most afternoons. "Hey, Spider," I yell sometimes. "Catch anything?"

Today I give her my line about fitting in. "We have to make our adjustments to society," I tell her, half-kidding, half-serious. I am also testing the waters of the River Mad.

"Know my advice to you?" Loretta favors me with a glance.

"What?"

"Never kiss a buzz saw."

"It isn't a buzz saw I'm thinking of kissing," I say to her. "It's Benny Soutar."

Loretta drops out of the tree, lands lightly on her feet. "Ooooh-la-la," she says, and I see we are friends again.

MARCIE NEVERS is the buzz saw. She is one of the popular girls, maybe the most popular, and she pretended to be my friend two summers ago when there was nobody around for her to talk to but me. When her real friends came back she called me up and told me her family was moving to Indiana and she was sorry but we would never see each other again. We said good-bye on the phone. I remember thinking it was funny she had never mentioned moving before. Then there she was big as life the first day of school, and when I went up to speak to her she cut me dead. D-E-A-D. In fact, she looked at my chest and whispered something to Caroline, and Caroline screamed and I just got out of there.

That afternoon I was back in the woods doing some crying when I heard a match scratch, and I looked up and there was Loretta trying to light a cigarette. "I assume that what I am witnessing here are tears of rage?" she asked me. I didn't know Loretta yet—she and her mother had just moved into the only house for rent in the whole town, the white one with the broken screens at the dead end of Etra Road—I wasn't sure I had even heard her speak before. I blubbered out the whole story because she surprised me, and all she said was, "So what?"

"So what what?" I said, annoyed, but that is what is so good about Loretta. She doesn't care what anybody thinks.

"Who cares? Who cares what a little chicken giblet with a charm bracelet says or does. Marcie Nevers is an A-number-one hole," she said, and I guess we made friends then and there. There is nothing like hating the same person to get a friendship started.

"IS SHE the best you can do?" my mother has asked. "Surely there is someone else in this town for you to be friends with besides that creature." Actually, what my mother holds against Loretta has more to do with Loretta's mother and their lawn ornaments than with Loretta herself, whom my mother has never troubled to get to know. Loretta's mother is the hostess at the Red Curtain Lounge, which is lower even than waitress in my mother's view, and added to that is their unmown lawn and the statues of Snow White and the Seven Dwarfs that adorn their front path, although all the dwarfs have been kicked over and Snow White has been missing since last Halloween. My mother was born in Philadelphia, and she would rather die than have a lawn ornament. "So tacky," she says, in her tired-out voice. So tacky so what, is what I say. Sew buttons on underwear. Loretta is the smartest girl in the school. They are going to have to give her valedictorian someday, which will kill them. She is reading The Book of Knowledge, straight through. I tell my mother this.

"The Book of Knowledge?" My mother rolled her eyes. "That is a pedestrian exercise if ever I heard one." You cannot win with my mother.

At least she never brings up the gossip. Word is that Loretta's mother was never married at all, that she got preggers and didn't even know which guy did the dirty deed, so she had to leave wherever she was and travel around before plopping down in this place, Lately, Iowa, population 374. Loretta used to say the picture on her bureau was her father, which is a man in an eye patch, but I know she cut him out of a magazine. Then she told me her father was blown up when a radiator exploded right next to him in Minneapolis, where they used to live. I thought that was a strange way to go.

Loretta's mother is littler than Loretta, and she uses words like "insist," and "fascinating," and she wears her hair in a French twist. "I *insist* you stay for supper," she said to me the first time I went over. I think she was so glad Loretta has someone to play with. We had fish sticks and ketchup, Loretta's favorite. "Brain food," said Loretta, tapping her forehead. "Good for the old noggin." Loretta's mother lets Loretta eat whatever she wants. If she wants fish sticks five nights in a row, that's what they have. Or squash. Sometimes Loretta just wants string beans for a month, that's fine with Mrs. Wilson. "The body knows what it needs," is her theory. "It all evens out in the end."

Saturday morning of Marcie's party I am in Loretta's house. We are lying on the kitchen floor playing Monopoly, and Loretta is unwrapping pieces of bubble gum and reading the fortunes. "You will meet a tall dark stranger," she says to me, winking. We are talking about Benny, and tonight. Loretta hasn't decided whether she wants to come or not. I half hope she won't. Then, right out of a clear blue sky, Loretta's mother says the strangest thing to me.

"Marjorie? I guess you have heard the rumors about me by now."

I don't know what to do. I try to nod my head and shake it at the same time, so she can choose whichever answer she wants.

"About Loretta's father. Mr. Wilson," she goes on, looking right at me. She has a can of fruit cocktail in one hand and an opener in the other. Loretta is on a fruit cocktail kick this week. "Well," she says, and to my relief she turns around to open the can. "The fact is," she says, "there was an incident." The way she says the word *incident* reminds me of those delicate tiny glass animals you can't put down hard. "Mr. Wilson, on occasion, drank to excess." I look at Loretta, but she is busy with bubble gum. I don't know what to do with my eyes, so I just sit there politely, looking at my lap. But she doesn't go on and on. "And I thought it best to leave," she finishes up. "Loretta was too young to remember him well, isn't that right, Loretta?" Loretta nods her head and stuffs three pieces of bubble gum in her mouth. "He was a very nice man, but he drank to excess and I thought it best to leave." She says it all again, all at once.

"Oh," I say, and I try to put a lot of meaning into it.

Then she dumps half a can of slippery fruit into one bowl and half into the other and gives them to us. "Since you are Loretta's best friend, I thought you were entitled to the truth," she says, and then she goes out of the kitchen.

Loretta and I can't figure out why she suddenly told me this, but after she leaves for work Loretta says I might as well hear the rest of the story. "He came home really late one night and he was smashed and thought he was in the bathroom and he whizzed on my mother in her bed." Loretta's mouth is full of gum, and I'm not sure I heard right.

"He what?"

Loretta takes the gum out of her mouth.

"He unzipped his fly and he took out his pecker and he widdled all over my mother."

"Wow," I say. "Holy effing cow."

"We left the next day before he woke up. She thinks I don't remember any of it." Loretta puts the gum back in her mouth and blows three quick bubbles, popping each one with a satisfying snap.

"So you lied about the radiator," I say.

"I rayed about the liediator," she says, nodding her head.

WHEN I tell my mother this story, which I really don't know why I do, she surprises me by throwing her head back and laughing. My mother has a loud laugh. She has to wipe her eyes. "Gives new meaning to the words 'pissed-off,' doesn't it?" she says. I have never heard her use the word "piss" before.

"It's weird, isn't it?" I say, getting carried away. "Loretta's mother left her husband and your husband left you." Then I notice my mother's expression. "And me, too, he left me too," I add, to soften it. "I don't mean really *left*," I keep going, but it's too late. "I know he's just on the road," I say. "It's just funny they're both gone, sort of." That's where I end up.

My mother's face has frozen over with that look she gets, you can watch it happen, like ice forming on a puddle. She doesn't say a word to me, she just gets up and smoothes her skirt and leaves the kitchen. Thing is, you name any job that takes a man away from home and that's a job my father has had. We don't know where he is anymore. I had a postcard six months ago, "World's Largest Vase," and he sent me a red enamel watch for my birthday. It has tiny hands and a picture of the moon, and it was so beautiful I almost popped it in my mouth. But the first day I wore it the enamel got scratched and I tried to fix it with nail polish, but it just got worse so now I keep it in my top drawer so he won't see it and get his feelings hurt in case he comes home.

My mother is in her room when I leave for Marcie's. I knock on her door quietly and I say, "I'm going now," but she doesn't hear. Or at least she isn't answering. When she gets like this it can last a couple of days. I am wearing a black skirt and a red belt and the yellow sweater she told me to throw out last summer when she noticed my development. "You need a brassiere," she said, and her lips made a line in her face. "And you'd better get rid of that sweater unless you want every Tom, Dick, and Harry following you all over town." I rolled it up in tissue paper and hid it under my socks. I am also wearing a pair of high heels she thinks she threw out. It is much easier to get dressed and get out of here when she is in a bad mood.

The party is in Marcie's basement. They call it a rec room because they fixed it up. It's the latest thing. My mother says a cellar is a cellar no matter what you do to it, but I'd say this looks like a rec room, with turquoise tiles on the floor and fish nets and corks all over the wall. And the lights are ship lanterns and there are portholes painted on the wall with fish swimming in the painted water. There are a million glasses of Coca-Cola on the table and potato chips and onion dip, and everything looks very pretty with the lights down low and Buddy Holly on the record player. Marcie comes running up to me like I'm her long-lost best friend and she whispers and points to Benny, who is standing in the corner talking to Ed. My heart pounds to see him. Marcie is acting like she's the owner, like Benny is some rare tropical bird she's captured and got here in her basement. This is because Benny is king of the hoods but is also very nice. He has sideburns and cowboy boots and big shoulders, and he hardly ever goes to school, and here he is and I know he likes me. Last summer he asked me out to the movies, but I was too young then, only eighth grade, because when I looked out the window and saw him coming up the walk and he was wearing an ironed white shirt and a belt and different pants, and he didn't look like Benny Soutar—he looked like a Bible salesman or something—I made Loretta answer the door and tell him I had just gotten sick with a fever of 102. "Poor Benny," she said after he'd gone. "He got all dressed up to take your chest to the movies." And we rolled around on the floor laughing.

But that was last summer.

I am half hoping Loretta won't show up and half wishing she was already here. I don't really have anyone to talk to. Eddie is talking to Caroline now, and Benny is all by himself. I don't know what to do. Eddie is a big pain, he snaps your bra any chance he gets, I can't see why anyone would talk to him. He has yellow hair and black eyebrows and bad breath, so he is always eating wintergreens. I can't stand him. Loretta and I invent deaths for those we hate. "We'll crack his brainpan," is our new favorite. We laughed so hard when we heard the term "brainpan." It made us both think of brownies.

I am just looking around for Loretta again when this tall thin girl in a tight black dress and gobs of makeup on comes in, and I realize this is Loretta. She looks terrible. "Well, I came," she whispers to me as she looks around.

"Loretta?" I say. "What have you got on?" I am almost as tall as she is in my mother's shoes, and I feel delicate and grown-up in these clothes, sort of like a cookie. I try gently to steer her into the bathroom. "Loretta," I say, very kindly, "you have a little lipstick on your teeth." Instead of wiping it off she just smiles wider, which makes me want to give her a slap. "Loretta," I say, very firmly, "you put too much stuff on your face. You look like a clown."

"What about you? What about your own face?" she says, which really gets my goat since I know how to apply makeup. Then she walks away and drinks five glasses of Coke in a row. Which isn't saying much since the paper cups are no bigger than the ones you get in the dentist's office when he wants you to rinse out your mouth. We are once again deep in the waters of the River Mad. Now I see she has a yo-yo. God knows where she stowed it in that dress, but I see her throw down a hard sleeper and she starts walking the dog. Caroline makes the cuckoo motion by her ear, and I know that if I don't talk to Loretta she won't have anyone to talk to here at all.

God damn it to hell.

Then they put on a slow song, and miracle of miracles Roy goes over to Loretta and asks her to dance. "Nonsense," I can hear her say, "you come up to my navel," which makes me want to burst out laughing but I can't, and I feel sort of drunk.

Next, Eddie comes over to ask me to dance, and you can't say no, you have to be nice to them in this situation, and so I dance with Eddie and he smells like shaving lotion, and he tries to twirl me around and his hand is sweaty and he is starting to hum. When the music stops I see Marcie is talking to Loretta. She is hopping mad that Loretta was rude to Roy, and she has a point, but now she is being rude to Loretta. A minute later Loretta comes over to me and Eddie, and she says, "You make your adjust- ments to society, I prefer to let society make its own adjustments," and then off she heads to the door. Eddie looks at me and winks. "A carpenter's dream," he says, nodding at Loretta, "flat as a board and easy to screw."

"You little pip-squeak," I say to him, and I hate it that he wiggles his eyebrows at me.

LORETTA IS halfway down the sidewalk when I call out, "Loretta!" She doesn't hear me or else she pretends she doesn't hear me, because she just keeps walking. "Wait up!" I yell, but then there is Benny standing right next to me.

"Hey," he says in his nice quiet voice, "stick around." He nods toward Loretta. "She'll be all right," he says. I look out the door. Loretta isn't even turning to check if I'm coming. She doesn't care if I come or not. "Listen," says Benny. His eyes are grayish green. "What do you say we take a ride? We can give Loretta a lift if you want to." My legs are all watery, and my voice sounds high and thin.

"When? Now?"

"Why not," he says, and he grins. "You busy?"

I shake my head. "Take me by storm, Benny," I have practiced saying in the mirror. "I'm a woman now."

Loretta is nowhere to be seen by the time we hit Branston Street in Benny's blue Hudson. "I think she cut across," I say, and my hands are folded in my lap. I feel it important to have good manners. His car is so clean, it's like a little room; the seat is soft and velvety, and we have a cigarette lighter that plugs in and a radio, and the heater is on. It's like a little home in here.

"You smell good," says Benny.

"So do you," I say, like an idiot.

We park on the grassy place out by the bridge where Loretta and I used to sneak at night. It looks out over the highway that goes clear across the country. Loretta and I would take our ciggybutts and her yo-yos, and we'd climb out on the overpass, and she'd swing her legs over the edge with her four yo-yos that glowed in the dark, a Parliament hanging out of her mouth as she made her adjustments, and she walked the dog, or she walked four dogs, and under us a car occasionally passed hurrying from one end of the country to the other, and Loretta, barely recognizable as a human shape under the dark Iowa sky, must have looked, lights dancing from each extremity, like a tiny new constellation, and I was in back, invisible too, holding on to her waist, lest she disappear up into the sky.

AND BENNY begins kissing my neck and by my ear and my cheek and then my mouth. His hands are going up inside my sweater, and I push them away, but he says, "Come on. Come on," he says, "this will feel good."

And it does, of course. It does.

SO FAR SO GOOD

Bunny is standing outside the Golden Eggroll in East Moralia, New York. It is raining lightly, a gray November afternoon. Getting dark already. Bunny has left her ugly blue rat fur coat stuffed in the trash behind the restaurant, and she is wearing now her beautiful denim jacket, the one she embroidered herself. Rainbows and unicorns abound, shooting stars travel the length of her sleeves. Bunny is running away. She is tired of winter. She is tired of her boring life.

Bunny has her thumb out, and she holds a sign that reads SOUTH. She plans to surprise her boyfriend Dave, who joined the army two months ago and is stationed somewhere in Florida. Bunny thinks they might even get married. It doesn't matter how old you are down there, Bunny knows. She's seen the movie *Great Balls of Fire*.

Bunny has recently smoked most of half a joint she stole from her mother's purse and eaten two bites of a hash brownie, the rest of which is in her pocket. She has that funny bubble feeling in her throat.

Before she left the house, Bunny poured a quart of milk down the sink. She took all the silverware, including the can opener and two spatulas, and threw everything into the woods beside the driveway. Bunny feels bad about this. She shouldn't have done anything so babyish. She didn't buy any coffee, either, as her mother had told her to. "Get some more, will you, Bunny?" her mother had said, holding up the nearly empty can. "Mr. Ickes is partial to coffee in the A.M." And she had padded back to her bedroom, and Bunny had heard a man's laugh. Her mother looked so damp these days.

Running away is a spur-of-the-moment thing, but Bunny thinks she should have done it long ago. She wonders when she'll start to see the difference in climate, which state will start to get warmer. How many days it will take. She knows for certain only that Florida is hot and sunny all the time, with those huge red flowers and vines. You can swim at Christmas. She'll marry Dave. She'll get a job. She can become a waitress and save up money and open her own restaurant. Or a tattoo parlour, she thinks, remembering the embroidery needles in her pocket. She could learn that.

An Oldsmobile Cutlass slows down, stops. It is a shabby green car, the paint sanded off the driver's door. The driver rolls his window down a couple of inches. Bunny can't see his face, raindrops cover the glass. "Where you headed?" he asks. His voice is soft. He sounds handsome. Bunny steps closer to the car. "Florida?" she says, and shakes her sign. Bunny is fourteen years old.

"I can take you across the river," he says. "Into Jersey." He lowers the window another couple of inches and Bunny sees he is a little handsome. He has blue eyes and dark hair and a really nice nose. Bunny likes nice noses. Her own nose sticks up a little at the end and when she gets the money together she is going to have it fixed. Bunny takes another step closer to the car to try and see inside. The rain is starting to come down harder now, Bunny imagines fat little boxing gloves made of water pummelling her head and shoulders.

"Take it or leave it," says the man, and he shrugs. The car seems warm and cozy. "Thank you very much," says

Bunny, and she runs around the front as he leans over to open the passenger door and hold the seat down so she can climb in the back. The seat is wide and roomy although the window is small, and Bunny settles herself gratefully, arranging her possessions. She lays her sign carefully on the floor so as not to wet the upholstery, and places her knapsack next to it. Bunny has a great many Oreos in her knapsack, as well as three bologna sandwiches, $137, and a roll of quarters she stole from her mother, who stole them from work. These are in case she has to call somebody from the road.

"Set?" asks the driver, and turns in his seat to extend a warm dry hand toward Bunny, who shakes it gravely. He is wearing a leather jacket that squeaks like a new shoe when he moves. "Name's Gary," he says, and Bunny sees now that the whole right side of his face is purple. She tries not to notice, but it looks so velvety. Like a thin purple flapjack laid across his cheek.

"I'm Bunny," she says, and hopes he doesn't think her rude for staring. But Gary's eyes are focused on the red heart Bunny embroidered on the pocket over her left breast. For a second it feels to Bunny as if he is staring right through her clothes to her naked boob, but she realizes this is probably just the grass. Bunny doesn't really like to smoke, but she knows if you do it a lot, it gets better.

"What is that?" asks Gary, still squinting at her jacket.

"A heart," says Bunny. "I embroidered my whole jacket." And she holds out her arms to show him the stars on her sleeves. The moon on one cuff.

"Very nice," says Gary. "Very, very nice. You do all this work yourself?"

Bunny nods proudly.

"Well," says Gary, and he smiles at her. One of his front teeth is faintly brown. "Well. I've got a little artist in the car. Have to drive real careful." Gary's jacket squeaks again as he turns frontward. "Picked a bad night," he says, as thunder crashes nearby and he drives the car back onto the road.

"Really," says Bunny, and she looks out the side window. The rain is coming down in earnest now. She is lucky. She got a ride in the nick of time. She fishes out her mirror and her lipstick. Her mascara didn't get smudged in the rain, thank goodness, so she wasn't standing there like an idiot with makeup running down her face. She does need a touch-up of lipstick, though, and applies the pinky magenta color to her mouth. She can never keep it on. Bunny's aunt told her to apply a layer of lipstick and then pat it with powder and apply another layer of lipstick, but this has never worked for Bunny. Two minutes later and she always has her same regular boring lips again. Bunny peeps over the compact in time to see Gary's eyes in the rearview mirror looking at her. She hopes he doesn't think she was checking to make sure she didn't suddenly have a big birthmark too. She is glad she wasn't doing anything gross, like sucking her thumb, that babyish habit Bunny still indulges in when nobody is looking. Bunny's mother no longer tries to break her of this habit. "Go ahead, Bunny," she says. "Walk down the goddamn aisle with your thumb in your mouth." Bunny wishes she could stop, but she doesn't even know she's doing it herself, half the time. But her nail is all ridged and deformed, and she has a red bump on the joint, a callus, really.

Bunny puts her lipstick away and leans back in the seat. She pats the upholstery softly. It has buttons on it, and those nice pleats, and the car smells good, sort of like a chocolate bar. She closes her eyes for a second, and it's like she's floating. The tires make a swishing on the road, and the windshield wipers go back and forth, back and forth. Bunny opens her eyes. She thinks she should talk. Otherwise Gary might think she is thinking he is like her chauffeur or something.

"This is a really nice car," says Bunny.

"Yeah?" says Gary. "You call this nice?" His voice sounds friendly. Bunny watches as they pass a little blue Nova.

"Well, it's so comfortable," she continues. "And everything."

"Built for it, these old cars," says Gary. "You mind if I smoke, Bunny?"

"Oh, no," says Bunny. "Not a bit."

"Maybe you'd like a cigarette yourself, Bunny," he says.

"Thank you very much," says Bunny, breathing into it. "I'd love one."

"Light it for you?"

"Yes, please," says Bunny.

Gary puts two cigarettes in his mouth, and Bunny watches him light them with a silver lighter that snaps shut. He passes one back over the seat.

"Thank you," she says, and smiles at him in the rearview mirror. The cigarette is a Pall Mall, the kind her father smokes. Bunny takes the tiniest of drags. These cigarettes make her dizzy, and she hates getting tobacco in her mouth, but it would make her feel disloyal not to smoke it, as if she didn't love her father. And it might hurt Gary's feelings, too. Bunny wonders where her father is right now, and what he is doing. The last time she saw him was when he was packing to move, over a year ago. He almost forgot to take the necktie she had embroidered for him, black with a million snowflakes. It had fallen to the floor behind the bathroom door. Poor Daddy, she thought, with no one to take care of him.

"How many earrings you got in that ear?" Gary asks her. He must be able to see her really well in the mirror. Bunny touches her right ear. "You mean this one? Six. Three in the other."

"Never had an earring myself," says Gary, shaking his head. He holds up his right hand. "Only jewelry for a man is this." He wiggles his little finger. "Pinky ring," he says. Bunny sees a black stone in a gold setting.

"It's really nice," she says, and Gary puts his hand back on the wheel. "My friend's brother has this snake," she continues. "It eats these frozen baby mice? They come in a package. They're called pinkies," she says. "I think it's such a funny word."

"Knew someone had a boa constrictor once," says Gary. "Named it Mother. Hell of a name for a snake, huh? Mother."

"Really." Bunny tries to talk past the new bubble in her throat. She hopes she isn't making a fool of herself. The mice just popped into her head. "There is very little future in being a mouse," Bunny's mother had said when Bunny told her about the snake. Bunny notices the ash on her cigarette needs tapping and she opens the ashtray on the door. There are many butts in it already, red lipstick marks on their white filters. Bunny opens her window a little to throw her cigarette out, and turns to watch, but the rain extinguishes it right away so she doesn't get to look at the rolling ball of sparks on the road behind.

"You ever eat there?" asks Gary, pointing to a Taco Bell they are passing.

"No," says Bunny. "Never."

"Mexican," says Gary, shaking his head. "Dirty food."

"We usually go to Kentucky Fried," says Bunny. "I really love fried chicken." Bunny realizes she is hungry, very hungry all of a sudden. "Is it okay if I eat in your car?" she asks. "I've got some bologna sandwiches if you want one."

"Go right ahead," says Gary. "Make yourself at home. Nothing for me, thanks anyhow. Bologna doesn't sit well in my stomach."

Bunny eats two sandwiches. Then she takes five Oreos out of her knapsack and puts them in her lap. She used to separate the halves of these cookies and scrape the icing out with her teeth, but now Bunny puts the whole cookie in her mouth at once. This way she won't make any crumbs. She sits back with a cookie in her mouth and looks at the back of Gary's head. He is almost handsome, except for his cheek and his tooth, and maybe his chin is a little small. She almost doesn't care where he drops her off, she wishes they could drive around all night maybe. Bunny hasn't got much of a plan. She has a page torn out of her old seventh-grade social studies book, the map of the United States showing the different groups of states in different pastel colors. The southern states are pink, the Middle Atlantic ones are blue, and the Northeast, where Bunny is still stuck at the moment, are pale green. She can see how far she has to go on this map in inches, but no roads.

"You got a route in mind?" asks Gary. It's like he can read her thoughts.

"Just south," says Bunny, swallowing.

"I-95 is a big road," says Gary. "Catch it about any-where. Take you the whole way down."

"That sounds good," says Bunny. She is licking the crumbs out of the corners of her mouth. "I was consider-ing that."

"You going to Disney World?" he asks. She sees his eyes in the mirror.

"Oh, no," she says. "I'm meeting my boyfriend in the Everglades. He is a captain in the army. We are thinking about getting married at Christmas." Bunny doesn't con-sider this an actual lie. "He's been wrestling alligators down there," she continues. "They pay him to."

"You don't say," says Gary, looking at her again.

Bunny nods. "I almost went to Disney World once," she adds, to be polite.

"Well," says Gary, "as the man says, 'close, but no cigar.'"

Her father had been going to take her, but he never showed up. Her mother had been so mad. She had made plans to go to Las Vegas with her boyfriend, but every-thing had to be cancelled because Bunny had nowhere to go. Her mother wasn't going out with that boyfriend anymore. Now it was Mr. Ickes. The other guy had come to fix their dryer, which had a lint trap that kept catching fire. Bunny's mother turned everybody into a boyfriend, it seemed to Bunny.

"You must be wondering how come I'm running around loose," says Gary. "Am I right?"

"Yes," says Bunny. "I was." For a second she isn't sure. Was that what she was wondering?

"Fox like me."

"Yes," says Bunny.

"Fact is, I left my girlfriend this morning," says Gary.

"Really."

"Yessir, I've had quite a morning. Red-letter day."

"You must be sad, then." Bunny wonders what it would be like to kiss a man with a half-purple face. You would have to keep your eyes closed totally.

"Should have seen the look on her face," says Gary, "when I told her I was going."

"Poor her," says Bunny. She can't think of anything else to say. "What's her name?"

"Renée. But don't you worry about old Renée. Probably sitting around right now with her mother trashing yours truly. Their idea of a good time."

"Really." Bunny opens the ashtray again on a crack. Maybe these were Renée's cigarettes. Such red lipstick.

"So where I'm going is to my ex-brother-in-law's house in Jersey. Hoist a few."

"Well," says Bunny. She shuts the ashtray. "That's good you have somewhere to go."

"She wasn't so bad." Gary's voice sounds softer. His eyes are looking at her again in the mirror. "She just wasn't enough woman for me, you know what I mean?"

"I guess so," says Bunny, and she looks out the window for a minute. "Sure."

"So what about you, Bunny, you got a story to tell?"

"No," says Bunny, and she shakes her head.

"Come on," says Gary. "Girl like you taking off for Florida just like that? Come on. You got trouble at home, Bunny?" He is looking at her again.

"No," says Bunny. "Nothing."

"Your mother know where you're going? Your old man?"

"Well, I don't live with my parents," says Bunny. "I'm too old for that. But I'm planning to send them a couple of postcards when I get down there."

"Is that right?" says Gary.

"Yes," says Bunny, her face pressed against the glass. "It is."

Bunny's problems are all inside Bunny's head. She gets terrible pictures in her mind. For instance, there is a NO PARKING sign loose on a pole near where her mother works. Bunny has noticed it hanging off one bolt and when the wind blows, it clanks and bangs and crashes around. It looks to Bunny as if it might go sailing off one day, and she has imagined it flying through the air and splitting her mother's skull exactly in two, like a meat cleaver. This thought always makes Bunny touch her own forehead, finding the exact center with her fingernail. Every time Bunny has passed the sign she has meant to remind her mother to be careful crossing Front Street on a windy day, but she has always forgotten. Bunny thinks she might be almost like a murderer for not having warned her mother. Bunny will be sure to drop her a card from Florida, telling her to watch out.

Bunny digs at the center of her forehead with one fingernail. It feels good, finding the middle like that. She wonders if it might not feel sort of good to be split right down the exact center of your head. Then she wonders if having this kind of thought means she is crazy, or going crazy, and she takes a sniff inside her shirt. Crazy people smell funny, her mother has told her. So far, so good, thinks Bunny.

"Know any funny stories?" asks Gary.

He is really reading her mind again.

"Well," says Bunny, "this man falls off a roof."

"Yeah? You call that funny?"

"Wait. He falls off this roof that's like sixty stories high. There is a person on every floor sitting by the window, and as the man goes past each one they hear him say, 'So far, so good.'"

Silence.

"Get it?"

"I don't think it's funny."

"Neither do I. It's my mother's favorite story though."

"Stupid guy for falling in the first place," says Gary.

"Right," says Bunny. "But maybe he just slipped."

Bunny has imagined the man, looking like her father, standing close to the edge of the roof. Maybe he has a glass of beer in his hand, maybe not. Maybe he thinks he sees somebody he knows, which is really just a very small cloud. Maybe he takes one step in that direction and falls off the roof. Maybe the building is like totally tall and he never has to actually land. Maybe a place will open up in the ground and let him fall right through the earth and out the other side, and there will be like a net in China that will catch him softly, like a hammock, and he will live there happily ever after eating moo shu pork and getting healthy and tan. Maybe he'll give Bunny a call and she will come live with him there. Anything can happen, thinks Bunny. Really.

Gary has swung the car off the road and is pulling into a gas station. "Getting low," he says, turning in his seat. Bunny yanks her thumb out of her mouth. "You want a Coke or something, Bunny? You want to stretch your legs?"

"I just need to use the ladies' room," says Bunny, and Gary unlocks the door and pushes the seat forward and Bunny climbs out. It has stopped raining for the moment, but it is cold, and Bunny wraps her arms around herself as she crosses the blacktop into the bathroom on the side of the gas station. The small room is dirty, paper towels all over the floor, and Bunny holds herself above the toilet to pee. She washes her hands in hot water, and finding nothing to dry them on, wipes them on the seat of her jeans. She looks in the mirror. She looks so white in this terrible light. She takes out her lipstick. She wants to write something like Bunny Loves Dave, but she is afraid maybe the mirror has germs that will get on her lips later so she just does her mouth again and puts the lipstick back in her pocket. She looks around, but there is nothing to take, no little clean piece of soap as a souvenir of this first stop. The door slams behind her, and she walks quickly to the car. Gary is ready to go. She must have kept him waiting.

"Sorry," she says, climbing in the back again.

Gary starts the engine, and they ride for a while down a dark country road. Bunny doesn't see any lights, really, and hardly any other cars.

"Where are we?" she asks, after a while.

"You cold, Bunny?" says Gary, as if he hadn't heard her. "You cold, you might find a blanket under the seat back there." Bunny isn't cold, but she thinks she should pretend she is to be polite. "Right under the seat," says Gary.

The blanket is there, and as she unfolds it, something falls into her hand. An earring. A little pearl earring. Bunny doesn't know what to do. She doesn't like that her heart has started to pound. She takes another small piece of hash brownie and puts it in her mouth. She needs to change the horrible mood she is getting in.

"Did Renée wear earrings?" she hears herself ask.

"Time to time," says Gary. "Time to time. Why do you ask?"

"I don't know," says Bunny. "I was just wondering, I guess." She wishes she had said, "Does Renée wear earrings?" Not "Did Renée wear earrings?" It makes it sound like Renée is dead. She hopes Gary can't read her mind right now. This always used to happen to Bunny when she smoked grass. She wound up thinking somebody wanted to kill her. Even Dave, once. "Bunnybunny-*bunny*," Dave had said, taking her face in his hands. "Not what I had in mind at all," and he had slid his hand inside her shirt. They had never gone all the way. "You're jailbait, Bunbun," he had said to her. "Got to draw the line somewhere." She had been thirteen when they started making out, Dave nineteen. But he respected her, that was what was so good about Dave. He respected her. But then he had gone and joined the army.

Bunny looks out the window and sees they are nowhere. No lights at all, not even through the trees. "You know what?" she says, in a high voice. "I think maybe I should get out soon. I mean if that's okay. Are we like near Nyack or anything?" Bunny is still holding the earring, and she drops it quickly into the ashtray.

"Car doesn't make stops in Nyack," says Gary, and he laughs. "Just kidding. Fooled you, didn't I?"

"You did." Bunny nods her head vigorously.

"You know, Bunny," says Gary, "not every day I get such a pretty little passenger. I was fixing to adopt you, maybe. Would you like that, Bunny?"

"I already have a father," says Bunny carefully. "And a mother."

"I was kidding," says Gary.

"I know," says Bunny. "I was just playing along." She puts her hand in her pocket with her embroidery things. She touches the small pair of scissors, fingering the sharp curved point. What she thinks of as the teeny beak.

"You a Gemini, Bunny?" asks Gary.

"No," she says. "I'm not."

"Could have sworn you were a little Gemini. What are you then? Taurus? Pisces?"

"I'm embarrassed to tell you because it's so boring." Bunny is relieved to be having a regular conversation again. "I'm a Capricorn. See? I told you. It's like being nothing."

Gary doesn't say anything, and Bunny wonders if maybe he is a Capricorn. Maybe she has put her foot in her mouth. "Except for a guy," she adds hastily. "It's totally cool for a guy."

"You don't say," says Gary.

Bunny's right hand is feeling between the seats now. She is looking for the other earring. Instead, she finds something made of some thin material that turns out to be a woman's stocking. Just one. A stocking. Bunny is now pretty sure that Renée is dead, that Gary strangled her with this stocking, and that thousands and millions of dead neck cells have been dislodged and are flying around in the car right now. She closes her mouth to avoid swallowing some. She shoves the stocking back between the seats. She feels cold, and sick to her stomach.

"We're getting there," says Gary, "in case you were wondering." He sounds cheerful. "Took the long way 'round. Safest route, in this kind of weather. And tell the truth, Bunny," says Gary, smiling at her in the rearview again, "I enjoy your company."

"Well," says Bunny. "Thank you. But I know it must be getting pretty late." She wonders if he can tell her voice is shaking. "You must be in a hurry, and I really should get out in Nyack and call my dad. Or anywhere. Tell him I'm safe and where to pick me up and everything." Bunny has no idea where her dad might be or even if he has a phone anymore. "I didn't mention before I was going to meet him, I guess."

"Oh-ho," says Gary. "Dear old dad, huh?"

"Yes," says Bunny. Tears are coming out of her eyes, although she isn't crying. "I really have to try and call him up. Where are we? I think I need to get out of the car right now."

"Now isn't that like a kid," says Gary. "Are we there yet, Daddy? Are we there?" Gary uses a thin high voice. Bunny is silent. "So, Bunny," says Gary, "tell me the truth. What do you make of the face?"

"The face?" asks Bunny. "You mean your face?"

"That's what I mean," says Gary, pulling a pair of sunglasses down from the vizor. He puts them on, twists in his seat briefly toward Bunny, then he turns frontward again. "A fox? Or what."

Bunny doesn't know if Gary is joking or not.

"A fox," she says. "A definite fox."

"And what about the grape stain?" Gary's voice is rising. "What about the purple ink? What about the whole right side of my goddamn face?"

"It's not so bad," says Bunny. Her heart is pounding again, and she has to catch her breath after she speaks. He probably never even had a girlfriend named Renée.

"You tell me something," says Gary, slowing the car down. "This isn't so bad," he points to his cheek, "how come I got no date for Saturday night?"

Bunny doesn't know what to answer. "Well," she finally says, "it's only Tuesday. Maybe you'll meet somebody."

"How about you, Bunny? Want to go to the movies?"

"Well," says Bunny carefully, "I'd like to but I'm supposed to be in Florida."

"Oh, yes," says Gary. He sounds sarcastic. "That's right."

There is silence in the car broken only by the sound of tires on the road. Bunny is afraid of this silence. She is afraid she might fall through it and disappear, like a hole in the ice. Gary pulls over to the side of the road.

"Why are we stopping?" she asks.

He doesn't answer.

"Gary," she says, her voice getting loud, "I think I'm

going to throw up back here. I think I better get out of the car," and Bunny starts pushing against the front seat.

"I could use a little company up here," says Gary, as if she hadn't spoken at all.

"I mean I'm going to be sick right in the car," she says. "Just let me out a second, I'll come right back, I promise."

"Getting pretty lonely up here," says Gary. "No telling what might happen I don't get a little company soon." His voice sounds friendly. "That's all I'm asking. A little companionship in the front of the car."

Maybe Bunny is blowing everything out of proportion, as usual.

"Just climb over the seat," he says. "Just sit up here next to old Uncle Gary. That's a girl."

Gary sits still while Bunny climbs over the seat. She sits next to the door, as close as she can get, and she stares out at the road ahead. It isn't really a road. They are in the woods somewhere. No lights or cars anyplace.

"Bunny." Gary speaks her name so softly it is almost a whisper. "Bunny, look at me." She turns her head and sees he is smiling at her, sitting still, so still, and after a moment she sees his penis sticking out of his pants, sticking straight up in the air. His penis looks to Bunny like it glows in the dark. Maybe he painted it with something to make it look like that. She turns her face away. She closes her eyes tight.

"Bunny, you mind if I masturbate?" asks Gary. She looks at him again, she can't help it. His left hand is already around his penis, and he gives himself a little squeeze. "You mind, Bunny? This going to bother you?"

Bunny nods her head. Then she shakes it.

"You don't have to touch it," says Gary, "you don't even have to look." Bunny closes her eyes again, and Gary's jacket starts to squeak. Bunny feels so calm. Like in the list of terrible things that can happen to you, this is not so bad, Bunny is thinking. He isn't making her do anything. And it's his car, after all. Her fingers fool with the scissors in her pocket. She imagines stabbing him somewhere, blood shooting out of him, hitting the ceiling, falling back in the car drowning them both. Bunny doesn't move or hardly breathe. If she breathes, the car will certainly fill up with blood.

Gary is making such sad sounds, as if he is crying. She remembers the peaches in her daddy's kitchen that got spoiled because he forgot to eat them. He was too lonely to eat by himself, Bunny thought, and she felt so sorry for him. "Don't waste your tears," her mother always said. "I don't see him beating a path to your door." But Bunny had felt sad just the same.

"You want to get out now?" Gary is asking. His voice sounds sad and tired. "You want me to drop you somewhere?"

Bunny shrugs.

"You want out? I can drop you in Trenton. I can take you to Trenton you want to catch yourself a train." He fumbles in his pocket and pulls out a roll of twenties. Starts to give her a few. "Really. Let me help you out."

Bunny thinks and thinks.

"In or out, Bunny," he says more sharply.

But Bunny can't make up her mind.

It is so hard to decide.

PART TWO

JUST MARRIED 1959

Buddy got a haircut and I really did not know him. From the back he looked like a bald-headed boy who had walked into church by mistake. Later I found out he cut it himself using one of those gadgets you buy from the back of a magazine. Buddy likes to save money. He didn't look like Buddy at all, but I had to marry him anyway. I don't know what would have happened if he had had short hair three months ago. I don't know if I could have fallen in love with a boy if I could see his actual scalp.

It was like marrying a total stranger.

When it was over and I had a ring on my finger we drove back to where we already live, which is the top floor of a divorced woman's house. On the way I saw a white horse and made a wish, but it was just that Buddy's hair would grow back quickly, which was the waste of a wish, since it will anyway. Usually when we drive I sit practically in Buddy's lap and he takes my hand and puts it on his leg, way high. So I sat close and put my hand there myself, but he just let it lie. I didn't know how to get it back, so I faked a coughing fit and then I fixed my hair with it.

"We've been married twenty-five whole minutes," I told him, when we had, but he didn't say anything back. He made one of those "uh-huh" noises, which never sounds friendly. "Everybody cried the whole time," I said next, "even me. I don't know why."

"No kidding," he said, and then it began to rain and he turned the windshield wipers on.

I hate where we live, to tell the truth. I know it's just for now, but my heart gets a sinking feeling when we turn down the street. The house has three floors of black furniture and brown carpeting and one huge gold mirror on the landing I am afraid will crash down and kill me on the spot. I always run upstairs. Plus, there is no telling when Mrs. Languidere is going to pop out and tell you something you do not care to know, or worse, when she is going to be crying somewhere you can hear it really loudly. Mr. Languidere left her seven months ago for a girl in the mattress department of Strawbridge and Clothier. I am sorry for Mrs. Languidere, but I don't want to hear any more stories about her horrible husband and the mattress queen, as Mrs. Languidere calls her. Mrs. Languidere says to call her Christine, but I just can't. She is about thirty-seven years old.

Yesterday she was right on the bottom stair crying her eyes out again, and I didn't know what to do. I couldn't just walk past her so I stopped and put my hand on her shoulder. She reached up and patted it, but she never stopped crying and finally I went out the door.

The trouble is, there isn't any outside here. There are just big expensive houses, and nobody walks on the sidewalks. I feel funny unless I have a destination. Penn Fruit is twelve blocks away so I walked there to buy our surprise wedding supper. Frozen lobster tails. We are not allowed to cook here, but Buddy's Aunt Dot gave us an electric frying pan that I plug in in the bathroom, and I was going to boil them in that. Of course Buddy fell asleep sideways on the bed when we came home married and did not wake up even when I told him we had a feast. So I ate all four tails all by myself. Ha ha.

I met Buddy on the boardwalk of Point Pleasant in the

state of New Jersey. He had just shot 202 wooden ducks in a row, and I was standing very close to him, and when they gave him the big teddy bear he turned around and gave it to me. He was very handsome. I was wearing my red wraparound skirt and a little sweater. Then he bought me a hot dog and we found out we went to almost the same college—his is only five miles from mine. He is a sophomore and I am a freshman. Was. He asked me if I liked to swim, and I said the ocean here was warm as pee. I told him I came from Massachusetts, which has a proper cold ocean, and I told him all my ancestors were whaling boat captains, which is not exactly true, although you never can be sure. Some of them might have been. He told me he had smelled me behind him, that I smelled sweet, like cotton candy. We started to go out in the fall after we got back to school. In fact we went out every single night for two months, and one night I lay down with him on his bed and one thing led to another, and he asked, "Is it okay?" and I didn't want to hurt his feelings so I said, "Sure," and it turned out that one time made me pregnant, which was my first time, which was either very good luck or very bad luck, depending on how you look at it.

It was terrible when I told my parents. I still think of

their sad faces. I was sitting on the couch, but nothing looked familiar. My mother had to get right up and go into the bedroom, and my father followed her while I waited to see what they would say when they came back. My father asked me, "How long?" and I said two months. "Do you love him?" my mother asked.

"Oh, yes," I said, "with all my heart," which was a lie, since sometimes I am not even sure I have a heart. So it was decided to get married right away. There really wasn't anything else to do, under the circumstances. What should I do about school was the next problem. My father said to tell the truth. "Tell the dean," he said. "That's what deans are for."

So I did. The dean said she was proud that I had been so honest but that I had to be out of the dorm in two weeks, and I could not take my meals with the other girls anymore. Who wants to? The meat they give you is all gray, and I never could get used to being served by girls who were just my age. I was used to getting up and getting my own food. And anyway, what did she think? You get pregnant from using somebody's fork? But she just looked at me over her desk, and her teeth were very long and brown, and she said, "You realize your education is over now." I think she said that because I was acting so happy as if I did not care one bit. I had to act that way, nobody has ever told me I could not eat at their table again. When I told my mother, she took my college jacket and she cut it up in little pieces, and then she threw it out. She didn't have to go that far. We could have just scraped off the crest.

NOW WE are living in Buddy's hometown for the summer so he can work and save up money for the baby. He will go back to school some day. It's important that he finish his education, and *his* school did not kick him out. We live in a tiny cute white house near his father and his Aunt Dot. Aunt Dot gives me advice. "Be patient," she says. "It's harder for the boy in this situation. The girl gets all the hormones." It is hard to be patient. Why should I be patient? I feel like throwing things at him. Either he is at work or he is going out for a quart of milk and coming home at three in the morning. It's like Buddy has a whole life here and mine has been left behind. He sowed his so-called wild oats, and now what am I supposed to do? Lie around like some stupid field?

Last night we finally went for a walk together. We were even holding hands, like before we got married. And it was a pretty night, and the sky was purplish black with stars, and I was liking how the air smelled. Then a car full of boys drove up and slowed down, and one of them stuck his head out the window and yelled, "Fuck her! I did!" and then sped away. I felt so terrible. I felt like it was true. Buddy acted like it was true, too. He wouldn't speak to me all the rest of the night. I began to wonder if it was true, which is a sure sign of craziness. My name is Virginia Davenport, and I never slept with a living soul until Buddy came along, and that is that.

My ex-roommate Sylvia called me up, but I was sorry that all she could talk about was the French professor she was in love with and also who was going out with whom. And the biology assignment that she failed. I tried to sound interested, but after all there is a living being growing inside me and my interests are much deeper now. So after a while she hung up, and I took a little nap. She failed the hard-boiled egg. That is what we were dissecting when I got pregnant. Not the exact moment, of course, the same week. Personally, I didn't care to know that much about the hard-boiled egg, especially when you might be eating it the next day. That awful part is the actual brain of the chicken-to-be. "The snotty part," is what Buddy calls it, but I wish he wouldn't use that word. Also, *piss*. I think *piss* is a very ugly word, and I don't see why he has to use it so often. *Pee*, I think, is fine. "Girls pee," says Buddy. "Well, horses piss," I said, but he seemed to like that.

The other night we were driving, me and Buddy and Chick and Irene, who are his old friends from high school. We had a bunch of beers, and so the boys got out and they peed by the headlights. They were writing their names in the sky with their own urine, and Chick yelled back to Irene, "If this stuff were phosphorescent you'd see some pretty fancy signatures!" Irene and I were back in the tall grass by the red taillights peeing away to beat the band, and then Buddy yelled back, "Sounds like a couple of cows back there," and I was so embarrassed because by that time Irene was finished and it was only me. Peeing a hole clear to China. But Irene didn't tell. We wiped ourselves with leaves.

You have to pee all the time when you're pregnant, something I did not know before.

The baby has started kicking. It is exactly blip blip blip in my stomach. Buddy says this is impossible. He used to be premed, and he thinks therefore that he knows everything. He says the embryo is no bigger than a lima bean at this moment and what I am feeling is gas.

Gas. What a disgusting word.

And it is not—this is my body and I know what I am feeling, and I have never had this particular sensation before in my life. I recognize it as the tiny kicks of a tiny new person, whatever Buddy may think. He isn't sticking to premed anyway. It was all Dot's idea. Buddy would like to be a country-western singer and ride a cayuse all his life if he had his way, which he does not. "On my cayuse," he sings night and day when he's in a good mood. When he's in a bad mood, which is most of the time, he doesn't sing or whistle or even hum. My mother had a friend who always hummed, and my mother wondered why her friend was so depressing to be with, and finally she realized her friend was always humming "Taps." I think that is so funny, but Buddy just looked at me. Well, too bad for him if he has no sense of humor.

I keep thinking of the baby now as a lima bean. But I know it is not, it has a little face and maybe still that little tail, although I hope not. I will be happy when it no longer has a tail. It gives me a funny feeling to have something inside of me that has a tail.

SOME DAYS I am so sleepy I don't even get out of bed until the afternoon. Then Dot and I go to the flea markets. I bought two old pewter spoons for three dollars, which Dot said was a good buy. Buddy said it was too expensive. Next time I'll say they were a quarter each. Then Dot and I were sitting on her couch. She likes to drink Benedictine out of little yellow eyecups and sometimes I have a swallow with her and Buddy just glares at me. He should talk. He is not the boss of me.

I am the boss of me.

I just don't know what to tell me to do.

Dot herself is no longer married. "Widowed," she says, which sounds like "widdered." She says fry-pan instead of frying pan, and hamburg instead of hamburger, but she is a very nice person. She practically raised Buddy. I'm not sure whether she's his real aunt or his adopted one. She says if she were marooned on a desert island she would be able to make a complete and nourishing meal out of just a bottle of ketchup. I said, "Oh, no, Dot, that would be awful," but she went home and came back later with a pot of just that. Ketchup soup. It was so sad and terrible, and I had to drink a cup of it, although I managed to get rid of most of it in the plant. "Delicious, Dot," I told her.

Dot has a wrinkled face from being outside so much in summer and very skinny arms. Her husband died naturally, but she is terrified of choking to death and advises me to cut up everything into very small pieces. "Although you can choke to death on a piece of popcorn," says Dot, "or a dried pea." "You can't be too careful," she is always warning me. Dot drives an old Studebaker with no paint on one door and broken chairs in the back and dog hair all over everything. She has three dogs, all of them brown.

Sometimes when I have fun with Dot it makes me feel so bad for my own mother. When I laugh at Dot's jokes I wonder if my mother would be sad that I'm sitting around all day with somebody else's relative, as if my own mother were forgotten. But I have to be somewhere, don't I?

On the weekend Buddy drops me at Dot's while he goes fishing with Chick. I don't see why I should be stuck at home while they have all the fun. "Slippery ravine," says Buddy. "Can't have you sliding down into a heap in the river. I'll bring us back a mess of fish for supper," he says, and he smiles, and so I say, "Okay, go ahead." But does he? Ha. When he comes home you can see he's had a few beers and the only thing he has caught are three tiny little fish he should probably have thrown back according to law. "They are pathetic," I say, looking at them swimming in the pail. "You should have given them back their freedom." So he gets mad and kicks the pail over and walks into the house. Sometimes I hate his guts, I really do. Poor little fish.

"They don't have feelings," says Dot, as she helps me pick them up. "They have such tiny little brains."

"But they look so terrible flapping around," I say.

"No, I meant men," says Dot, and we laugh our heads off. Then I stay over at her house and we have a little Benedictine, and I did not go back for an hour and a half. Buddy is asleep of course. He is always asleep or out. He likes to be anywhere but where I am, it seems to me.

WHEN I told Buddy I was pregnant he did not say one word. It was raining, and we were double-parked, but the engine was running and we were supposed to be going to the movies. "I'm pregnant," I said. He sat very still, and then he reached over and flipped off the windshield wipers. His words sounded stiff when he spoke, as if they were made out of some sticky material and it was difficult for him to get them out of his mouth. "What do you want to do?" he asked me. He did not look over at me though. I shook my head. I did not know one thing to do except get married. "Do you want to get married?" he asked then, but it was not really a proposal. "If you don't mind," I said. "I'm really sorry."

"Don't worry about it," said Buddy then, and he reached over and squeezed my hand. "It's okay." And I have to say this was nice of him. Some boys try to run away.

But he is not turning out like a regular husband. He never notices if I get mad or pays any attention. He would never fold me in his arms if I were upset. He never knows what to say, either. "I love you," try, or "I'm sorry," try, or "Can I get you a cup of tea?"

My father is different. He says please and thank you to my mother. He's called her dear and darling all his life, and anyone can see he loves her to death. When they dance together she takes her glasses off and it's very romantic. If she burns the meat he tells her it is delicious that way, too.

Yesterday we went to Irene's. I think she was Buddy's girlfriend once, but I like to go. She lives next to a hot flat field and bees hang around and it smells dusty and sweet. Irene and I sat on her porch swing while Buddy and his friend Chick went to the farmer's market. Irene asked me so nicely how I was feeling. We talked about what a hot summer this is and what to name the baby and also Irene's plans. She is going to secretarial school when she has saved enough money. I told her she could have my typewriter, but she already has one. She acts sometimes like I am the poor thing, not her, when it is me who has a husband and poor Irene will have to be a secretary.

Sometimes I feel like an invalid when Irene tries to wait on me hand and foot. "Let me get it for you," she says, or "Buddy, get your wife a cold soda," which she doesn't understand will put him in a bad mood. He likes to have his own ideas. I don't even want a cold soda. It makes me sick to my stomach.

Chick and Buddy like to tell dirty jokes. I know this is how they always were, but Buddy is married now and I don't care for this kind of talk—especially when I am pregnant and sitting right in the room. "I hope you know your baby is hearing every single word," I said. And everybody looked at me. "What?" said Buddy. "I just don't think it's funny," I said, and everybody got quiet. Irene got up to make popcorn. Then Buddy started telling the joke again. I got up and went out by myself and sat on the front porch. I could see the Big Dipper, which is exactly the same Big Dipper I looked at last summer when I was home. They put on some music inside, and I heard Irene laugh. After a while Buddy came out on the porch. "Come on back in, Virginia," he said. "It's getting buggy out here." He said it in a nice voice, but I don't think he felt nice. I know somebody sent him out to get me.

So then I went back, and Irene passed the onion dip, and nobody said a thing. Then Buddy burped and Chick burped, and that started a whole burping contest with Irene's stopwatch. I had to pretend it was very funny, but really I thought it was digusting. Chick won. He could say "You have white teeth" five times in a row while burping. Buddy has white teeth. He has the whitest teeth I ever saw on a person not in the movies. But so what, is what I say.

Now I am trying to list the good things about Buddy. He is nice to Aunt Dot. He washes her floors for her and does her grocery shopping if she is laid up. I love Buddy for this, but why can't he be nice to me, too? If it looks like rain, Buddy takes all Dot's sheets down from the line. This is because Dot has one leg shorter than the other, and if she misplaces her shoe, or once the dog ate it up, and it was hard for her to get around—Buddy helped her all that week. "Dotty," he calls her, and makes those pretend punches at her arm, which she loves.

I asked Buddy if Dot was a blood relation. This was because of her leg. I would not like to have our baby born with one short leg. He said she wasn't, and he thought I was nasty to ask. I didn't mean to be nasty. I just wanted to know. What is so bad about that?

SOMETIMES WHEN the baby kicks I get so homesick. It is such a funny feeling, I can't explain. Not homesick for a place exactly, just a homesick feeling.

IN THE afternoons I wonder what my mother is doing, so I look at the clock. Four-thirty. She is probably having a cup of coffee and getting ready to fix supper. Today I called her up. Just for a few minutes—it is very expensive long distance. "What are you doing?" I asked her.

"This minute? I'm scrubbing potatoes for your father's supper. How are you, Virginia, how are you feeling?"

"Buddy loved your recipe for leg of lamb," I told her.

"Did you make the little roast potatoes?"

"I did."

"Did they work out? Did they get brown this time?"

"Perfectly. Buddy said it was the best thing he ever ate."

"Oh, that's so nice," my mother said. "You always were a good little cook."

"What are you having for supper tonight?" I asked her, although I knew perfectly well. It's Saturday. Home fries and a ham omelet.

"Home fries and a ham omelet," said my mother. "It's Saturday."

"The baby is kicking," I told her.

"Really? Oh, that's lovely, Virginia. Kicking already."

That's the nice way to talk.

"Do you need anything?" my mother asked. She always asks this.

"No, we're fine, Mom." I always say this.

We never even tasted the potatoes. Buddy hates jelly with his meat, it turns out. And the worst thing was the meat was bad, I had kept it too long in its wrapping. Buddy didn't take more than one bite, and I wound up throwing everything away, which was wasteful, I admit that freely. But I don't see why he had to make such a huge deal of it. I told my mother he loved the lamb and ate up every last potato, and then I felt so terrible for her.

She would hate to know how much I lie.

MAN & WIFE

Buddy has a pimple and I don't want to kiss him. He says this should not matter to me. He says he is my husband and if I really loved him I would kiss any part of him no matter what. I know what this really means. He is not talking about just any part. I know what he is talking about. But I don't want to. I just don't, that's all. I don't see why I should.

We don't have intercourse now, because I told Buddy the doctor said it's too close to the baby, which was almost true. Some doctors do say that. What Dr. Foley actually said was that if I don't get myself a good bra I will have breasts like an African. "If you want to wind up on the cover of *National Geographic* with tits down to your knees, that's up to you," were his exact words. I could not believe my ears. When Dr. Foley looks at me my eyes water, it's so embarrassing. I'm not crying, I'm not even sad, but my eyes just start tearing to beat the band.

Everything is proceeding nicely with the baby. I love being pregnant. I love to be so big, like another planet, so bulky and delicate at the same time. Sometimes when it is so hot the only tolerable spot left in the universe is the kitchen floor, I lock the door and pull off my dress and lie down on the cool linoleum, naked, on a tablecloth, with both fans blowing right on me. I watch my big belly move, like a sack of live fish.

We have only been married five months and the baby is due in September, which has all the busybodies counting on their fingers and to them I would like to say go to hell, but I mind my manners. Anyway, I am looking forward to the baby. I have all the little bottles of lotion and powder and the tiny little undershirts and blankets, and I unscrew the tops of everything and smell and screw them up again. Everything smells so sweet. If it's a girl she will be Martha, and if it's a boy he will be Jesse, after Jesse James, who was one of Buddy's ancestors. Maybe this is why I fell in love with Buddy, because of Jesse James. Everybody else at college was walking around like their bodies were nothing more than a stalk for their heads, only Buddy was handsome and strong and smart all at the same time. He had curly black hair, and when anybody said anything funny he would stiffen and throw his head back, as if he'd been shot with a bullet. Then he'd double up laughing. I liked that. I liked that he loved country western and his ancestor rode a horse and carried a gun. My ancestors were just plain. I would like to have Apache blood, or French.

So I got pregnant.

Before I met Buddy I had a boyfriend who went to Holy Cross. Jack Connery, who would not pet. When he came down for winter weekend I took his hand and placed it inside my sweater (we were kissing in his car and I had already undone the buttons myself), and he left it there exactly three seconds and then he took it away saying, "Some things are better saved for marriage."

How wrong he was.

To tell the truth, I liked it better before, when we didn't do it. I liked trying not to do it, almost doing it. I liked it better in cars when your breath sounded like something inside you had broken. I liked not doing it better than I like doing it. After a while the novelty of lying down full length with a boy on a bed wears off. It just wears off. And then what have you got? Poking around. Or worse. And Buddy acts like there's something wrong with me if I don't feel like doing something he feels like doing. Why should marriage change everything? If I didn't want to do that before, why should I want to now all of a sudden, just because we're man and wife?

Man and wife. It sounds so strange. I don't feel like a wife, it's embarrassing to use the word. I feel like a fake wife, I don't feel like anybody's actual real wife. I don't know what I feel like. Yesterday I even forgot I had a new name, which made me feel so guilty. So I sit on the back steps and I say the words. "Wife," I say, "wife, wife, wife." I do believe there are secrets locked up inside words if we could just find the can opener, so to speak. "Husband," I say next. "Husband." But all I can come up with is that I like the word "wife" better. It sounds so slender. "Husband" is an ugly word, like "warthog."

I look at the laundry on other women's lines and I wonder how they get it done so early, and what they are all doing now, back inside. I decided to wash the bathroom sink today, using a pair of Buddy's socks. I planned to rinse them out and hang them up afterward, killing two birds with one stone. But the socks left a trail of blue hairs on the porcelain and then they were too slimy with Ajax to rinse properly, and I wound up throwing them out. I hid them in a paper bag, and then I put coffee grounds on top so Buddy will never find them. He comes home sometimes in a bad mood from painting all day. He straightens the cover on the couch in an angry way or points to the dusty windowsill. "What do you do all day?" he asks. I really don't know.

I'm miserable today because of the fight we had last night. I made a big turkey dinner and a yellow cake with chocolate icing, because it was five months to the day since we found out I was pregnant. And I set the table with all our wedding presents including the candlesticks, and when Buddy finally rolled in he was three hours late and half in the bag. He was accompanied by Chick Freund, who goes out with Irene, who I recently found out was Buddy's girlfriend in high school. I was mad and I asked him did he know how long it took to cook a goddamn turkey and how inconsiderate he was to be so late, but Buddy started to laugh for no reason, I could see he could not help it—he looked at the turkey and he looked at me, and he just could not or would not stop. I saw he was digging his fingers into his palms the way I do when I try not to laugh, but it wasn't working. I did not see what was the big joke and told him so, but he laughed more and had to lean on the table for support as if he might collapse and die laughing. So I said if he did not stop I would probably go ahead and have the baby there and then on the floor and Chick looked nervous. "Buddy, I think you better eat something," Chick said, which was nice of him, but Buddy was shaking his head from side to side, tears coming out of his eyes by this time. "Haw, haw, haw," were exactly the sounds he was making like some animal in a barn.

So I went directly to the kitchen and got a roll of tin foil and started wrapping up the entire table, turkey and all, singing "Mine eyes have seen the glory," I don't know why, it is my favorite hymn. Then Buddy started rocking the rocker with his foot, which he knows I believe to be bad luck, and then he took a spoon and began dinging a glass, which I have told him will kill a sailor for every ding, so I got a glass of milk and threw it at him. He stopped laughing right away.

Then he called me a name no husband should call his wife and I told him to shut up, which I also should not have said, and Chick said he would be going, but Buddy left first. I grabbed his sleeve, but he shook me off and just went out the door all soaking wet with milk and I screamed, "I hope you die!" when I realized he was actually leaving, and "I hope you both die!" when Chick followed after. I slammed the door and sat down in the blue chair and wondered if Irene was in the car. Then I went into the kitchen and banged my fist down on the cake. Anger is like a brand-new emotion now. It is like a kitchen appliance that arrived without instructions. I know it does something, but I don't know how to work it yet.

I WOKE up when he came in, it was around 2:00 A.M. I heard him cleaning everything up, which I had just left there. I kept my eyes closed when he finally came into the bedroom, hoping he would lean over and touch my hair or kiss my brow the way they do in the movies when they are too shy to tell you to your face that they love you. But he didn't. He just fell asleep with all his clothes on. In the morning he went to work before I woke up. He did not leave me a note or anything, just his coffee cup rinsed on the drainboard.

Maybe Buddy wishes he were married to Irene. The

first time I met her, Buddy and I were in line at the Acme and I was looking at the checker's hair, which was piled up on top of her head like egg white, with two fluffy pieces that stuck out at the sides, and I was imagining that my mother would say she could tell from her hair that life would be a disappointment to this girl, life just would not measure up to the expectations of hair like that, when the girl stopped adding our groceries and Buddy said, "Hey, Irene," in this quiet voice and I realized he knew her. She did not say one thing, and I remember her hands were shaking. "I got married. I guess you heard," he said, but did not introduce me. She flicked her eyes at my stomach.

"In the nick of time," she said.

"Be nice," said Buddy. "Be nice, now." He didn't sound like Buddy at all. He sounded like a grown-up.

"Fuck you, Buddy boy," she said, and threw the orange juice at him, which he caught and held tightly before putting it down. Then she finished adding up and Buddy put everything in a bag, and nobody said another word until Irene turned to me and said, "Good luck," and she smiled at me and I saw that one of her front teeth was slightly brown.

"Did you go out with her?" I asked Buddy as soon as we got in the car.

"Yes, I went out with her."

"Well, do you think she is pretty?"

"Who, Irene?"

"That's who we're talking about, isn't it?" I had my hands folded in my lap.

"She's all right."

"What about her hair?"

"What about her hair? What is this, Virginia, twenty questions?"

"I'm just asking," I said. "Did you love her?"

"This is the silliest conversation we have had so far," said Buddy, which made me very mad, and I did not speak the rest of the way home.

But I guess Irene has made her peace with it, because we've been out driving together all four of us a few times. The other night when Buddy and Chick went into the Blue Pinto for a pack of cigarettes, I asked Irene if she was still in love with Buddy. She said she didn't know. I told her about Jack Connery, and how sometimes I will be standing in the kitchen and his face will come into my mind, it's so terrible. I still think about him. I do not know what to do with these thoughts. I know I should not have them. That night I said to Buddy in bed, "I love you," and he said, "Uh huh, you don't act it," and I said, "How don't I act it?" and he said, "I don't know. You just don't." Then he turned on his side just when I was hoping he would make some kind of move on me. I felt terrible. Even though I don't really want him to, I want him to want to. Now we don't really touch each other anymore. If we brush up against each other in the hall we say, "Excuse me," like strangers on a bus.

The trouble is, I think he may love Irene. I think I like Irene better than I like me, so why shouldn't Buddy? She is so much realer than I am, I think. She offered to get me a job at the Acme, but we will be moving away from here when Buddy's school starts up again in the fall. This is only where we are for the summer. But she was so nice to ask. I could not tell her there was no way I could ever work at the Acme. I didn't want to hurt her feelings. Irene says she likes to work. She is saving up for secretarial school. She says the thing about being married is you spend all day waiting for your husband to come home and then when he does, it's no big deal.

How does she know this? She's not even engaged.

She is also brave, another reason I like her. She put a kitten out of its misery after Chick stepped on it and I had to go wait in the car. Irene should have been a nurse. Buddy did not look at me the entire time it was happening—Irene holding the poor thing underwater—he kept his face turned away, which may mean that he loves her and had to hide it. I know I could never have done what Irene did. I don't think I have any courage in me at all. I want Buddy to love me, but I think it would be like loving a piece of pound cake and he'd get tired of it after a while. So now I want there to be an accident so I can cradle the victim in my arms like Irene, so Buddy can see how good I am, too.

But anyway, so what. He is married to me, not her, and I'm the one who's pregnant after all, and right now I am so mad at him I could spit. I am not going to say one thing to him when he comes home. I am not cooking him any supper either. Let him cook his own damn supper. Let him eat crow.

When I hear the car I have barely any time to grab a book and sit down pretending to read. I am not going to look at him even when he comes through the door. Not even when he stands next to my chair. I just wet my finger the way he hates and I turn the page. Buddy will have to crawl upside down and backwards to apologize to me for last night. I can see the knees of his jeans out the corner of my eye. "Ahem," says Buddy, as if we are in a joke together. Then he bends down and puts a round white stone on the pages of my book. It is a lucky stone, a line runs right around it. "I remember you said these were good luck, so here. It's for you," he says.

At first I cannot speak at all. I cannot even swallow correctly, it makes a click in my ears. "Oh, thank you," I finally say, and then it all comes tumbling out. "Thank you, thank you so much, it is so beautiful and lucky, too, oh Buddy, thank you so much."

"It's just a stone," he says. "Don't have a conniption fit." But there is a smile in his voice. "Do I have time for a shower before we eat?" he asks, which he has never done before, this is really like a big apology.

"Sure, Buddy, of course," I say, and get up and go into the kitchen to make his favorite food, which is fried bologna. I am making little snips so they won't swell up like flying saucers when I hear him come out of the shower and flip on the news. "Frigging Pirates," he says, sitting on the arm of the chair with a towel around his waist. I come and stand next to him a moment. The Pirates are his favorite team. Mine is the Orioles, but only because I love to say it, Oriole. On Buddy's back and shoulders are all these droplets of water, and his hair looks curly against his head before he combs it out, and I have this crazy desire to lick the water off his skin. I reach down and touch his back, thinking, *this is my husband's back, this is my husband*, but he reaches up to rub where I am touching. "Cut it out, Virginia, it feels like something crawling on me," and he turns a second later to smile but my hand has flown from his back and I don't want him to think he surprised me or hurt my feelings.

Back in the kitchen I ask, "Want a beer?" and my voice sounds so normal and casual. "Want a beer?" I ask again, because he hasn't heard me, and my voice feels separate from my body and the words are separate from my voice, how peculiarly they hang in the air before dissolving, while I wait for his answer.

BABYSITTING

Irene has a baby sister who is not right. Her front teeth stick straight out between her lips, and one of her eyes rolls up inside her head so the white part shows when she gets excited. Her name is Pearl. I think that is such a sad name for her. Irene asked me would I watch her for an hour so I said yes. Irene used to be Buddy's girlfriend. I never knew of her existence until we moved here last month. This is Buddy's hometown. I am from Wellfleet, Massachusetts.

Irene dropped her off and said, "Just turn on the television, Pearl loves to watch TV, it doesn't matter what." Pearl wore a white sundress with straps, and she was dragging a little popped green balloon on a string she would not let go of. Irene put her down on the couch and flipped on the TV and said she would be back before too

long. She said watch that Pearl didn't swallow that balloon. She had been chewing on it all morning.

As soon as the door closed I got right up and turned off
the television. I did not think it right to plop a four-year-
old child down in front of daytime TV. I had a bunch of
magazines lined up to show Pearl the pictures and chocolate chip cookie mix in the kitchen for later. I planned to
have a tea party with Pearl. This is what I will do for my
own child, in case she is born a girl, which will happen
next month. I am very big now.

I sat on the couch next to Pearl and opened the magazine. "Cake," I said, pointing to the Betty Crocker Golden.
Pearl tried to pull the page out of my hand, but I said,
"No, Pearl, mustn't tear the magazine," and she stopped.
"Lady," I said next, turning the page. "Frying pan. Refrig-
erator." I took care to pronounce each word slowly
because I don't know how much Pearl understands and I
have never heard her talk. She hums mostly. It sounds like
"Begin the Beguine," but that's impossible. I have never
been by myself with Pearl before. I only see her when we
go over to Irene's. Pearl loves to ride on Buddy's shoulders. She touches his ears as gently as if they were potato
chips. Buddy is so good with her. He trots and gallops,

and Pearl just laughs and laughs and sometimes her eye rides up, but it always comes back down again. It won't get stuck up there no matter how fiercely Buddy jumps. That is just an old wives' tale.

Sometimes I am afraid that Buddy still loves Irene. This is partly because he never actually asked me to marry him, it's just that I got pregnant last spring and it was Buddy who did it. I hope he loves me. But he looks at Irene as if he knows her so well, and his voice is sweeter and friendlier than it is with me. He says this is all in my imagination. He says he is my husband after all, he married me, didn't he? But he never actually says in so many words, "I love you," and he never ruffles my hair when he goes past my chair. There are no little signs of love, which worries me.

But I have made my bed and must lie in it.

Pearl is afraid of the face on the Vermont Maid bottle. Irene told me this last week, but I never believed it until today. There it was in an ad on page forty-seven, and Pearl just started shivering and put her face in my sleeve. Maybe she thinks there is a woman's head floating in the syrup, I don't know. "It's okay, Pearl," I said, and turned the page. "Don't worry. There's nobody's head in the bottle." I sat still and stroked her hair and said, "It's okay, Pearl," a few more times because I liked how it felt, her hiding against my arm. I remembered I used to be afraid of my shoes when I was little, the kind that laced up. I was afraid the holes were rows of eyes looking at me, and I would not go into the room where they were. If they were on my feet I was fine, my mother said, which was a blessing. I was thinking about this when I felt something wet on my arm and it turned out Pearl was licking my sleeve for what reason I cannot imagine. This gave me a funny feeling, and I got up to change my blouse. I wanted to scrub my arm where her saliva was, and I did give it a little wipe with cotton dipped in alcohol, I don't know why. I know Pearl is not catching.

When I got back Pearl was tearing up the magazine and sailing the pages to the floor. "Oh, Pearl," I said sternly, though in fact I did not care, "that wasn't very nice." She must have heard my fake voice because when I sat back down she began poking me all over, in the breasts, even in my stomach. At first I pushed her hands away nicely, but then she tried to climb into my lap where there was no room whatsoever and put her balloon on my cheek, and suddenly I said "*cut it out*" in a very loud voice, and Pearl jumped back and slid her thumb into her mouth and one eye rolled up a little, and she looked at me and I knew she could see straight through to my terrible soul.

I have a terrible soul. Its natural position is to be crouching. I am always falling short of goals I set myself. For instance, last summer before I went to college I volunteered in a hospital and I did not like feeding the old people. I did not like forcing the metal spoon between their soft lips and prying open their teeth. Then when I finally did get one of the old ladies to eat, the nurse yelled at me because I'd made her eat too much mashed potato and it turned out that was bad for her. To this day I don't know why. Sometimes I test myself. Virginia, I say, suppose you came upon a dying man with vomit on his lips. Could you kiss him so his last moment would be filled with sweetness? I could not. I am sure Irene could. Even if the vomit was all crusty, Irene could. I saw her drown a hurt kitten with her own two hands. She had no choice, it was suffering. I had to go wait outside in the car.

After I yelled at Pearl she got so still and I just closed my eyes for a moment, because I usually take a nap in the afternoon. I woke up to a gagging sound, and there was Pearl standing on the coffee table with just the string hanging out of her mouth and the balloon swallowed down her throat. I got up and grabbed her and held her head and took the string in my hand. I did not want to pull too quickly, I was afraid I might pull something out of Pearl's throat that wasn't balloon, but by now both her eyes had gone back in her head and her eyelids were fluttering, so I gave a little tug and another, and out came the balloon. I went right into the bathroom and dropped it in the toilet, and then I threw up a cup of tea and flushed everything away. Pearl was still in the living room howling and howling, and I wondered if anyone was listening, if they thought I was hitting the child. For one tiny moment I wondered what it would be like to slap Pearl. This is the kind of thought that comes into my head, I am sorry to say.

I came back and turned on the television, and it was amazing that right away Pearl stopped crying and turned to the screen. It was not even anything for kids—it was the Galloping Gourmet—and I sat down next to her and we both watched him chopping onions, and then Pearl fell asleep and I looked at her teeth up close. They are like pale watermelon seeds she is trying to spit out, but they never leave her lips.

I began to wish for Irene to get back. I wondered what I

would do if she never came back at all. Would I have to take care of Pearl forever? I shook my head. She would have to go to a home. "You would have to go to a home, you poor little thing," I said very softly so she would not wake up. Pearl is big for four. One of the straps on her dress was cutting into the soft porky part under her arm, but I didn't dare move her in case she might wake up. I covered her with a blanket so Irene would not know I had seen the dress hurting Pearl and done nothing about it. I began to wonder where Irene might be. She has a job at the Acme, but this is her day off. Sometimes I'm afraid she and Buddy are sneaking around together, but I would never call Buddy at work to check. Suppose he was out? What would I do? I would just die, I would absolutely die. Well, at least we're only here until September and then it's back to school. Buddy is going to finish college. It is important for him to get an education. Our parents are chipping in with our expenses until we get more on our feet. I will stay with the baby, of course. It beats homework, I have to say.

Around four o'clock I noticed the baby had not kicked for hours. I know this is natural, and I know that toward the end the baby gets very quiet, but it made me nervous and I poked my stomach to wake him up so I knew he was still alive. It took a couple of pokes, but I got him moving, which was a big relief.

I was dozing when Irene knocked on the door. "Reenie's here," she called. That is what Buddy calls her, too. He never calls me anything small. It is always Virginia. Buddy says he has known Irene for a long time, he can't change that fact. He says he can't suddenly change what he calls her to please me.

I wish he would change what he calls me, then. But you can't suggest nicknames for yourself, they have to pop into the mind of the other person or it doesn't count. But what can you do with a name like mine? If I look at the word *virgin*, I see a thin pale naked person with two tiny nipples, which are the dots of the *i*'s.

"What's eating you, Virginia?" asked Buddy tonight. I shrugged my shoulders. I don't know what's eating me from what's not eating me, to tell the truth.

Pearl kissed me good-bye this afternoon. Irene told her to say thank you, and I was scared she would suddenly start talking in whole sentences and reveal the truth, but she did not. Instead she came over and reached her arms up, and I bent down and she gave me a kiss. It was the nicest feeling, which is what is so strange.

"What's going on in there?" asks Buddy, rapping on the bathroom door. "You okay?" I can't tell him I'm just looking in the mirror again. I keep checking to see if there's anything on my cheek, since I keep feeling Pearl's kiss, where her teeth touched me for just a second. I look in the mirror with both lights on, but there's no mark. Nothing there at all.

BUDDY'S BEST WORK

Three swans dropped dead this week, and this morning there was a fourth on the street out front. Nobody knows why. Maybe they are choking to death, maybe it is a sign from God. At first I thought it was a big pile of newspapers just starting to blow away, but when I got closer I saw it was a swan with one wing spread out on the road as if it had tried to lift itself up. Poor thing. Already ants were in its eyes. I called Buddy to come quickly I was so upset. I did not know what it might mean right in front of our house and the baby due in three weeks. Buddy said all it meant was that he had to pick it up, which he tried to do, but the body kept slipping out between the wings, it was hard to get a purchase. Finally he dragged it up on the lawn. I said I'd call the ASPCA, but Buddy shook his head. "Virginia," he said, "it's as dead as a doornail."

That was the second thing today. The first was that Buddy saw me naked. He came into the bathroom just as I was climbing out of the tub. His mouth fell open and he said, "God. Sorry, Virginia," and I grabbed the shower curtain and wrapped it around myself and stood there like a big awkward package until he backed out the door. He hasn't seen me naked since July. I was so embarrassed. I don't know why, I'm not embarrassed by myself, I love my big stomach, but Buddy never likes to talk about it. Back when the baby started kicking, I said, "Quick! Feel here!" but he acted like he'd been burned and snatched his hand away. "I didn't know your stomach would get so hard," he said. So then I told him a lie, which was that Dr. Foley had said we couldn't have sex anymore. I am shy since we got married and I got so big. I was never shy before. In fact, I undid my own bra before Buddy even put his arm around me last year. I was a virgin, though. I had never gone all the way. I just loved the top part.

At breakfast I tried to act like nothing was different, like I'd never been naked a day in my life, which I did by taking tiny little sips of everything in a ladylike way. Buddy kept staring at my stomach, and he acted so nice, like he wanted to wait on me hand and foot. He said how much bigger I looked without my dress on. He did not use the actual word, *naked*. He said he never saw anything so big, how did I manage to stand up straight? He said what happened to my belly button? "It looks like a little nose," he said. He used the word *navel*, which I can't say. When I found out about the oranges I stopped asking for them. I thought it was *naval*, I thought it had to do with them coming here in ships. These are words I cannot say out loud: *navel, nipple*. Not even if I am by myself. It sounds too personal.

Anyway, he kept staring at me. I thought he was going to ask if I would lift up my dress and show him again. Well, he had his chance.

Then we had a fight. I have been saving his doodles as he calls them, I call them drawings. I think he is truly an artist. All he has to do is pick up a pen and a galaxy drops down on the page: suns, moons, stars, comets, a whole solar system. But Buddy gets mad if I notice something about him that he hasn't noticed yet himself, and he probably thought he was still making ticktacktoes. I can't help what I notice, but it puts Buddy in a bad mood. He hated it when I found two gray hairs down south and when I told him how he jiggles his leg in the movies during the love scenes. But today, to change the subject, I got the pile of scraps with his drawings on them out from behind the bread box. It's matchbook covers and snips from the telephone book and margins from magazines and shopping lists all covered with planets and stars. I should have known. He got all red and angry. "You're saving this stuff, Virginia? You mean you're running around after me and saving my trash?"

I have a way of smoothing my face so there is no expression on it at all, like making a bed very tight, and I did that and got up to fill the sugar bowl. All I could think of was how fat my arms looked poking out the stupid sleeves of my dress. I was going to give him a set of Magic Markers for his birthday (Buddy will be twenty next month), but now I just feel like breaking them all with a hammer.

Then I sat down again and asked him please to pass the salt, which he did without putting it down first. I cannot take salt from a human hand, it is very bad luck, and I reminded him of this fact and he put the salt down then, hard. A little spilled, and I had to pick some up and throw it over my left shoulder. He asked me if I needed anything from the Acme he could pick up on his way home. I did not think he was leaving so early.

I said, "The Acme." As if it were a stone in my mouth.
"Um. No. Thanks. Everything is all dented at the Acme."
Irene works at the Acme, Buddy's old girlfriend. One
night I dreamed I saw them sitting on a bench, and his
whole body leaned toward her like a flower and he almost
touched her knee. That dream stayed with me way into the
afternoon, like dye. I went through his wallet once. I kept
expecting to find a piece of paper with Irene's name on it
squirreled away inside, but all there was was one empty
plastic place where a picture used to be. I am sure it was
Irene's picture. I wish he would ask for one of me, but he
doesn't think of it and I'm too shy to give him one. I have
looked at his yearbook, too, over and over, the page where
it says about Buddy and Irene and the blue Studebaker
and golfing at midnight, which Buddy swears he can't
remember what that meant. Ha. I left my yearbook around
one whole week, open to the page about Peter Maloney,
but he never even picked it up.

He left in a bad mood. I asked him when could I expect
him for dinner and he said it depended, and I said on
what and he said the humidity and how long it took the
spackle to dry at Mulford's. He is painting the whole second floor. So I said well, around when. He made one of

those *aaagggh* faces and looked at the ceiling. "When you see me," he said, and left without taking his sandwich. I slammed the door on him, and then I watched through the curtain. He stopped to pick up the swan and put it in the trunk of the car. How can he say such a mean thing and do such a nice one?

In the beginning, I used to go with him when he painted. I'd sit on a chair while he worked, and he told me how he always loved the smell of paint and how he liked doing the walls because it was so relaxing not to have anything in his head but a little scrap of music. He said mostly what went through his mind was one line, over and over, "If you be my Dixie Chicken, I'll be your Tennessee Lamb." He said he liked to do white because if he looked quickly around, the windows were squares of color, he loved the bright green or whatever he could see outside. He said it was beautiful. That was back when he talked all the time. I told him once when he was nuzzling me under my sweater, I said, "Know what I see when you do that?" My head was against the car door handle and my feet were sticking out the window, but I was so happy and Buddy said, "Mmmph," because his mouth was full of me, and I said, "A whole barnyard full of chickens!" because it was true, and Buddy said, "What?" lifting his head to look at my face, "What?" but I don't tell him things anymore and he doesn't tell me things anymore. Maybe we've run out of things to say. We've known each other ten and one half months now. When he comes home I say, "How was your day?" like somebody on TV, and he says, "It was all right," and then there doesn't seem to be anything else really to talk about unless I make it up. Before we met and I got pregnant he was saving his money to take a trip across the country. Now he had to spend it all on rent and baby furniture, and we are living right where he has always lived. He never says anything about it, but sometimes he looks at me, and I know he wishes he were in Utah or Wyoming or California by himself.

I looked up swans in my book. Unlucky, just as I thought, but maybe that's only when they're alive. Maybe a dead swan is good luck, though I doubt it. I know peacock feathers are very unlucky and parrot eggs are terrible news, but maybe a dead swan is all right.

Last time I watched Buddy paint he was doing the baby's room. He was up on the ladder and there was nothing in the room but the ladder and an old drop cloth and a dopey little fan and Buddy himself. He had a cigarette in one hand and a roller in the other. It looked so lonely to be a man. Buddy says he does his best work alone. He doesn't even want a radio. He doesn't like me to come along now, it's like I am his big booby prize. He wants me to stay home and rest.

He called me at ten-thirty to say he would be home at six. I was not nice to him. "Fine. Great. I can hardly wait," I said, and hung up the phone. Then I felt terrible. He was only trying to apologize. So I took the Magic Markers and put them in one of our wedding present vases like a bunch of flowers, and I decided to walk over to Mulford's and bring him his lunch. Right on the way is the Acme, and I glanced over and there big as life, the worst thing, my worst nightmare come true, Buddy was standing over by the dumpster with Irene. Her hair is so pathetic and her fingernails are long, and she is so short. Once she said she hoped Buddy made a better husband than he had a boyfriend, and I said, "Why did you go out with him?" And she thought for one minute. "Because I can sing the first bar of anything and Buddy can sing the second." It was the first I'd heard of Buddy singing, and when I asked him he just shook his head. I am trying to learn the songs

Buddy knows, but they're mostly cowboy songs and they don't even play them on the radio.

Anyway, I saw them immediately, and it looked like he was about to kiss her, he was leaning down toward her the way they do when they are talking to itty-bitty girls and I thought he was going to practically kiss her, and then I felt so hot, which it was, ninety-two degrees, and I have to say I'm sorry but I fainted. First time in my life. I just sank right down in the parking lot. When I woke up Buddy's face was about two inches from mine, and he was asking are you all right are you all right about sixty times in a row. "What are you doing here?" he asked. I said, "I know you love her, you were almost kissing her, why don't you just go there, I hate your guts."

Buddy said, "Virginia, you have too much imagination." He said he was saying good-bye to Irene, because she was going away for several months. I said, where? He said to visit her grandmother. Well, that's a lie, she probably doesn't even have a grandmother most likely. But I was too hot and sweaty and I didn't really feel very well, and Buddy put me in the car and drove me home and then he stayed, he did not go back to work, he made me some iced tea and he had a beer, and I lay on the couch while he fixed the fridge, which has been leaking. I felt happy for no reason. I just liked lying there knowing he was in the kitchen and the baby was moving a little bit, an elbow maybe. After a while he came in the living room. He had the Magic Markers in his hand.

"Know what I want to do?"

"What?" I said.

"Do you really want to know?"

"What? I said what?"

"I want to draw on your stomach." His face looked so serious.

"My stomach?" I circled it with my arms.

"It's such an interesting shape right now." He kept nodding.

"My stomach? You mean on the baby?"

"Not on the baby. Your stomach. It's so big. All I could see all morning was your stomach, Virginia, even when I was painting the ceiling, I kept seeing your stomach. What can I tell you?"

"My stomach? What are you going to use?"

"Magic Markers." He held up his hand.

So I said okay. Buddy said he needed access to the whole canvas and we couldn't use the bed, which is too squashy, and the light in the bedroom isn't good. "I can't lie on the rug," I said, "I just can't. I need something soft." So Buddy blew up the air mattress using a bicycle pump, and I lay down on that with a pillow under my head.

He lifted up my dress and I closed my eyes, and he whistled. My stomach stuck up like a mountain, I know, I've seen it often enough. "Yegods," said Buddy. "Jesus."

"Your hands are cold," I said, which was a very personal thing to say, because it was like asking him to warm them for me. He rubbed them together for a minute. "Better?" he asked. "Fine," I said.

Buddy's palette was blue-violet and magenta and yellow, it was green and black and red. He drew planets and suns and stars and shooting stars and moons. I loved the feeling, that he was dragging color across me. The nibs of the pens tickled, but I got used to it.

"When can I see?" I asked him.

"Not yet." Buddy's mouth was working the way it does when he is concentrating. This is when I can stare at him as long as I like, because he does not notice. He has grayish green eyes with little lines in them, like very old ice, or a windshield that has cracked crazy but not broken. I love to look at him, but usually I have to cover up my feelings with a sheet of conversation or something.

"It's like leaning out of a rowboat and drawing on the bay," he said. I didn't say anything. The baby was not kicking very much.

"What did you do with the swan?" I asked after a while.

"The swan?" He was so absorbed he didn't look up.

"The swan. The swan this morning."

"Oh," he said, "the swan. I took it to the woods."

"The woods?"

"Over near the lake. I found a good place."

"You buried it?"

"Sort of. I covered it up. I got a lot of fallen branches and I covered it up." Then he got silly. He started imitating Al Jolson. "Swannee, how I love ya, how I love ya, my dear old swannee," he sang.

"Oh, Buddy, you're an idiot."

"Stop wiggling," he said. That was such a personal thing to say to me. It sounded so friendly and private. "And I can't concentrate with all this talking," but his voice sounded very nice.

"Okay," I said. "I won't say another word."

Buddy started drawing again, and we didn't say anything for a while.

"Remember Pegasus?" I asked him.

"Why did you say that?" Buddy stopped drawing, his hand resting on my stomach.

"No reason. He just popped into my head. I was thinking about stars, I guess."

"I was just drawing him," said Buddy. "That's strange."

"Maybe my skin knew," I said, "and sent a message to my brain." Buddy shrugged and went back to work. "Don't color in the whole sky," I said, thinking how hard this was going to be to wash off. "Good thing the baby is three weeks away," I was saying, at the exact moment, Jesus Mary and Joseph, that my water broke.

"What's going on?" asked Buddy, springing back, because it is like an ocean when that happens. "What's this?"

Well, he helped me up and we got a lot of towels, and he insisted on taking me right to the hospital, he would not let me do one thing. "I can carry that perfectly well," I said when he got my little suitcase, which had been packed for a month, but he wouldn't even let me carry my own pocketbook. "You just get in the car," he said. He didn't exactly kiss me when they took me away, but he squeezed my shoulder and gave me his sweater, because I was starting to shake from the excitement. I have never had a baby before.

"Who's the Michelangelo?" Dr. Foley wanted to know. All the nurses and interns kept coming in to see my stomach, they laughed and marveled, and I wished Buddy could have heard what they said, but husbands are not allowed in. When Maddie was born, I heard one nurse say, "Why, she's beautiful!" Which she is.

When I gave her to Buddy, the first time he really held her, I could see he was afraid her arms and legs and head might spill separately from his arms, but when he had satisfied himself that she was all of one good little piece, he let himself look at every part. I pretended to be taking a nap. I watched him turn her over and saw him find what I found yesterday: on her shoulder blade, which is no bigger than the back of a teaspoon, is the red outline of a wing, very faint. I watched him do exactly what I did yesterday. He wet his finger and touched it to the mark, but it did not wash off. Indelible. I already knew, but I did not say one word.

PART THREE

MODERN LOVE

Sometimes he comes up behind me at the stove and lifts my skirts and we do it right here in the kitchen like a couple of kids. Quite a change from Noah, who could only stay hard by imagining me being sawn in half. Robbie is the sweetest, nicest man I've ever gone out with. His back and shoulders are broad and strong and make me think of the word *wingspan*. When we go to sleep he folds me in his arms as gently as if I were an origami bird. But nothing is perfect. He is dead broke. And worse.

He burned his own house down. Well, not entirely down. He set fire to the living room and then he took a shower. Don't ask. It was late and he was watching basketball, and I was in New York and he was probably stoned. The candle must have fallen over when he got up. Anyway, when he opened the bathroom door ten minutes later he almost choked to death on smoke and was lucky to get out the bathroom window with his life. When he was little, Robbie had asthma and learned how to breathe through an opening no bigger than in those little plastic stirrers that come with a drink sometimes. That's how he escaped, using that calm.

Nothing much was lost, because there was nothing much. Robbie's wife took it all when she left him four years ago. He had a mattress, a rug, a color TV, and a kitchen table. Most of the damage to the house was smoke damage, but Robbie got a new mattress, which is in the living room. To get to it we walk on this plastic road Robbie unrolled from the kitchen. Robbie has always slept in the living room, at least since his wife left. He likes to live like a refugee. Everything in the house is filthy with smoke except the kitchen and the bathroom, which Robbie has cleaned. The only thing we can touch is each other.

Robbie had a business once with his wife, who made jewelry, but it all fell apart when she left. "I lost my designer," he likes to say, shaking his head. He does odd jobs now: hangs a door, paints a room; he used to deal, but I don't want to know about that. When he's really broke he takes to the streets with his fiddle (that's what he

calls his violin), which is how I met him. I had decided to
find my own true love once and for all, that afternoon, no
joke. I was tired of waiting for men who were sixteen
hours late. I took off my bra and headed up Broadway in
my silky red dress with the polka dots, and there on the
corner of 115th was a big tall galoot playing bluegrass with
a crowd of students gathered around tapping their feet. I
worked my way to the front and had a look. I liked his
shoulders under the T-shirt; I liked his long curly hair
and the intense expression he had on his face. I liked how
low down his jeans hung, and the silver buckle on his
belt. I found out later his wife designed it; it's in the shape
of a bird.

I thought he had noticed me and I knew it was one of
my better days, because a woman standing next to me
whispered, "You don't have a stitch on under that dress,
do you?" which gave me the shivers, and I went up and
dropped a dollar in the guy's hat. A Phillies baseball cap,
actually. He looked at me and smiled and said, "Can I
buy you a cup of coffee with that?" and I said, "What, my
own dollar?" and that was pretty much that. We walked
off together, and I must say I loved being the envy of all
those little undergraduates being as I am thirty-eight

years old in my stocking feet, but I can still reel them in now and then.

We went for a cup of coffee at Tom's Diner and wound up back at my place sitting on the sofa a sofa cushion apart.

"Did you read all those?" Robbie asked, pointing at my bookcase.

"Sure," I said, "more even," although I don't know why I felt like bragging.

"Far out," he said, and whistled through his teeth, so I leaned over and kissed him, I really couldn't help it, and he jumped me like I was food and he was starving. Which he was, which we both were. So then we started pulling our clothes off, and I said, "Come on, let's do this in the bed." And we did, stayed there two days. Then he hitched back down to New Hope. That night he hot-wired Ma Bell to give me a call.

"I love you already," he said.

You can't beat that.

MY MOTHER has asked only a couple of questions about my new beau. I can tell she knows this is something she doesn't want to know too much about. "But what does he do?" she asked me.

"Oh, this and that, he's a musician," I told her.

"Oh?" she said, in what I call the held-dripping-between-thumb-and-forefinger voice.

"And he's kind of a carpenter," I added lamely.

AT LEAST he looks like a carpenter. He looks as though he ought to be a carpenter. And he does a lot of sanding. He has tree trunks all over his backyard which he intends to make into lamps or tables even. In the garage he has a dozen broken stringed instruments of one kind or another which he has promised to repair for people who assume he can fix as well as he plays. He can't, hasn't the foggiest notion, but he hates to disappoint his public. He has pried open a couple of violins as if to peek inside. Very gingerly, very delicately. Reminds me of me as a kid trying to sneak up on my grandfather's Victrola and surprise the tiny man who lived inside. "What do you do when they want these back?" I asked Robbie. He shrugs. "Why don't you just tell them you don't know how to fix stuff?" He looks at me. "You don't understand the business world," is what he says. I am too nice to point out that I am the one making a living in the business world.

Well, not exactly a living, and not exactly the business

world. My apartment is rent controlled, so I can afford to work in publishing. I do freelance proofreading for a couple of university presses. Boring, but my schedule is my own. I do a little writing, too. Words have always been my stock-in-trade; I was raised on words.

Robbie is an ignoramus. The only book Robbie has read from start to finish is *Dune*.

My mother's first criterion for a man is that he be interesting. What this really means is that he be able to appreciate my mother, whose jokes hinge on some grammatical subtlety or a working knowledge of higher mathematics. You get the picture. Robbie is about as interesting as a pair of red high-top Converse sneakers. But Robbie points to the mattress on the floor. He grins, slowly unbuckling his belt, drops his jeans. "Lie down," says Robbie.

This is interesting enough for me.

I GOT down for the weekend two nights ago. Now that it's spring I come every Friday; he has a lawn, trees. When I arrived he was sick as a dog, his skin was so burning hot it hurt me to touch him. "For God's sake," I said, "don't you have any aspirin in this place?"

"Sit on me," he said. "It will make me better."

"Forget it," I said. "You need aspirin."

"Sit on me," he said again, "please." So I did and he rolled me over underneath and came right away, and the next morning he *was* better. At breakfast I spilled jelly down the inside of my shirt. Robbie stuck his tongue out as if to lick me clean.

"It's everywhere," I said.

LAST NIGHT he wanted to sleep outdoors in a sleeping bag. Sometimes the smell of the smoke gets to him. I agreed, but I was nervous about bugs and snakes and I thought I'd have to pee. Robbie cuddled me. "I'll keep you perfectly safe," he said, and I began to relax until I saw a possum running right next to us, and I screamed and made Robbie carry me into the house, where I insisted on sleeping in the kitchen with all the lights on, and Robbie didn't make a fuss.

"How could anybody leave you?" I asked him.

"Beats me," he said.

NOW AND then Robbie says something memorable, something I could almost tell my mother, stuck as she is on the well-turned phrase. I asked him if he thought I was getting too fat, since I've put on ten pounds since we met.

"Don't lose an ounce," he said, "I love it. You're like a big soft playground." Big soft playground. I like that. And once when we almost fell off a bench making love I asked him how he kept our balance. "All part of being a carpenter," he said. "You have to know the teetering point of everything." I collect these phrases like gold leaf.

Sometimes when I look him full in the face it shocks me how much love I feel. It's partly how his face lights up when he sees me coming. How he eats me up, lavishes me on himself. I am his one luxury. Lots of men nibble around the edges like you were an anchovy canapé. Not Robbie. He runs to grab me, lifts me up, twirls me around. I notice one of my feet goes up, automatically, just like in the movies. He is the only man as glad to see me as I am to see him. Who shows it. Even my husband never told me he loved me. "Love," he would muse, his head full of science, "what is it? A complexity of emotions, good and bad, not easily summed up in a single word."

"HOW IS Lars?" my mother asks from time to time. She always liked my husband. He knew a lot. "Fine," I say. "Why don't you call him yourself?" We have been separated seven years now.

"Do you still love your wife?" I asked Robbie the first night we met. He looked down at the backs of his hands. "I hope not," he said.

NOW IT is Sunday morning and I'm sitting at the kitchen table waiting for Robbie to get home for lunch. He is off "doing a favor for a friend." I declined to ask which friend, what favor. What I don't know won't hurt me. I've got pea soup cooking on the stove and a batch of cornbread almost ready to come out. The table is covered with bills this weekend, a whole slew of them so overdue that on some of these pieces of paper Robbie is named Defendant. It gives me a chilly feeling. "I'll never marry *you*," I say out loud. It frightens me to think of owing so much money. It doesn't frighten Robbie. I think having money frightens him. I think he figures what you don't have you can't lose. This morning he showed me the contents of his pockets. Thirty-five cents. "Is that all you have in the world?" I asked him. He nodded, showing off, I think. On the floor by my feet is a cardboard box full of coat hangers and two chipped mugs that say "I ❤ New Jersey." That's about it for the kitchen. Half a dozen plates.

My mother really would not get this scene. She doesn't

know that it's easier to play house when all the odds are against you. All my mother understands is snob. "I *am* a snob," she admits, "I'm a snob and I'm nasty. It breaks my heart to think of my girl doing laundry for a man whose name is written in script above his pocket."

That would be a step up life's ladder for Robbie.

THERE IS a knock at the back door, and I get up to look through the window. Standing on the porch are two police-men. Never have I seen policemen so close to where I have just slept and eaten breakfast. I open the door feeling like a crook, as if they are going to ask me why I am spending the weekend in a burned-up house with a dead-beat. But they are very nice.

They call me ma'am. They ask me if Mr. Halleck is at home and if I am Mrs. Halleck. No, I say, I am a friend of Mr. Halleck, and he is expected later in the day. They give me a piece of paper with a phone number on it and ask me to ask Robbie to give them a call. They touch their hats when they leave. Neither one has looked at my chest even though I am only wearing one of Robbie's thin undershirts, nothing underneath.

Then Robbie calls to say he's on his way. "Heat up

lunch," is what he says, to which I answer, "Want me to sit on the stove?" Then I tell him about the cops. He doesn't say anything for a second, a bad sign.

"Did you tell them where I was?" he asks.

"Robbie, I don't know where you are," I remind him. "I told them you'd be back later."

Sort of a choking sound. "Did you say when?"

"Robbie, I just said 'later.' They were perfectly nice, they weren't mean or anything. They just wanted to ask you a couple of questions."

There is another little silence on Robbie's end of the phone. I have lived long enough not to interrupt a silence.

"Connie. I want you to do something for me."

Uh oh.

"What?"

"Take all my stuff out of the dryer and throw it in a bag with my sneaks and meet me behind the A&P at two-thirty."

"What did you do?"

"Nothing, not a thing. A friend of mine is in a jam, and I don't want to answer any questions about him. I need to get out of town for a couple of days while this blows over. Maybe we could go up to your place."

My place?

"My place? What if they tail me home? My car is parked right out front. Maybe they got the license number."

"Connie, there are a lot of things you know a lot about but this isn't one of them. Please just do what I'm asking."

"Not until you tell me what's going on. What friend? The one you do favors for?"

"Two-thirty, Connie. I can't talk now."

I hang up the phone and sit at the table again. Shit. I have no desire to answer a knock at my front door and find New York's finest standing there. This is not what I had in mind. An outlaw is one thing, a jailbird is something else again. I look around the kitchen. Robbie has restored the walls, fridge, cabinets to their original shade of blue, a color they used to call aqua. Aqua is what you painted everything thirty years ago when what you really needed was a whole new life.

I pack up Robbie's clothes, sneakers. I fill a Thermos bottle with soup and wrap the cornbread in a clean towel (mine). Then I get in the car and head for the A&P. I am two hours early. I plan to leave his stuff on the cement bench behind the parking lot and get out of here. But there he is, early too, swinging his arms against the chilly afternoon. He hasn't seen me yet. Oh Robbie. How am I going to do this? I pull up next to him, he is surprised to see me, but he hides it well. I lean across the passenger seat to roll down the window, and start handing him his stuff through the window. "Ankle express, Robbie," I say. "Here are your clothes and some soup I was making." He is bent down, looking in through the window at me. "I think you're more than I can chew," I say, and I feel like crying so I keep very steady with my voice. I have really surprised him though, and he looks crushed for a moment, the quadrants of his face separating like a jigsaw puzzle whose pieces have turned to water, but he recovers quickly.

"It was nice while it lasted, Connie," he says. "I want you to know that."

"It was, Robbie," I say, "it was nice while it lasted." Then he smiles and shrugs and blows me a little kiss, turns around and heads for the highway. He doesn't look back. The man has pride.

I sit here absolutely still, cursing my rotten luck. Look at those shoulders, I think to myself, they could carry water for miles. "Oh, for Christ sake!" I yell, and bang on the steering wheel. I think about my quiet rose-colored apartment. I think about my kitchen, its fading picture of a watermelon slice, my cake forks, my grapefruit spoons. I suddenly think of something my mother said once of a long-dead friend of hers, someone she hadn't thought about in years. I remember how it chilled me as an epitaph. "She almost had a story taken by *The New Yorker* once," is what my mother said. I remember vowing never to let that happen to me.

So I put the car in drive, and I drive it over to where Robbie is standing on the road, his thumb out.

"Oh all right," I say, mostly to myself, and lean over again, this time to open the door.

A TOOTH FOR EVERY CHILD

Louise, who is pushing down the tall grasses near the land of menopause, accepts an invitation from Mona, who is not that far behind. Mona could use the sight of Louise. "I need a drinking companion," she says. Louise can hear the twins wailing in the background.

"We don't drink anymore," Louise reminds her.

"But we can talk about it, can't we? Remember pink gins?"

"That wasn't us, Mona, pink gins. That was our grandmothers."

"Don't quibble. Just get off the bus in Portland. I'll pick you up."

"I'll come Friday. Thursday I've got my teeth."

THE ONLY man in Louise's life right now is her Chinese dentist. Her entire sex life consists of his warm fingers in

151

her mouth, against her cheek. She thinks of them as ten slender separate animals, so dexterous is he. She is undergoing root canal, paying the coward's price for years of neglect. Every Thursday she settles herself in his chair and he sets up what he calls the rubber dam. Eyes closed, Louise imagines a tent stretched from tree to tree. Under this canopy he sets to work chipping and drilling, installing a system of levees and drains. He stuffs tendrils of gutta-percha in the hollowed-out roots of her teeth and sets them on fire, reminding Louise of the decimation of the tropical rain forests. She imagines bright green parrots flying squawking out of her mouth, lizards running up the fingers of her dentist. Loves may come and loves may go, but dental work goes on forever, thinks Louise.

"You owe me nine thousand dollars," says Dr. Chan.

"WE'RE HAVING a lot of work done," says Mona apologetically, as they pull off the country road and onto the rough dirt path that leads to the house Mona and Tony have built overlooking the lake.

"Aren't you embarrassed to be so successful?" asks Louise.

"It's not me, Louise. Blame Tony. All I've been recently

is fertile. Wait till you see little Joe. He is anxious to see you."

Mona and Louise have been friends for thirty years. Louise had her babies first, four of them; she has been married twice, divorced twice. Her children have all grown up and gone except the baby, who at seventeen is in Italy this summer. Mona's first child, Joe, is five years old. She has twins, Ernie and Sue, eleven months. Louise wishes she had had her children later, when she knew better; Mona wishes she had done it when she was young. The two women are comfortable together, and Louise is planning to spend the week playing with the kids, sunning herself on the porch, reading.

Tony is off supervising the tennis court ("the tennis court?" Louise has repeated, incredulous), and Mona and she and little Joe are in the kitchen, Joe nestled in Louise's lap. Joe is learning about where babies come from. Mona is horrified to discover he thinks babies and peepee come from the same place, and Louise has taken it upon herself to explain about the three holes. A hole for peepee, a hole for poopoo, and the babyhole. "The babyhole is just for babies," Louise explains, proud of her succintness. She had told her own children, years ago, that she had made them all by herself, out of a special kit. "What is the babyhole used for when there aren't any babies?" asks little Joe, not unreasonably. Louise looks mournfully at Mona. "Well, not really much of anything," Louise says, "in a bad year." Mona bursts out laughing, and the two women cackle until their noses turn pink.

"The place is crawling with workmen," says Mona later. "You always wanted a guy who worked with his hands, remember? And the roofer is really quite choice. Fifty-three. Good hands."

"Do you talk like this in front of Tony?" asks Louise.

But it is the boy who catches Louise's eye first. Standing beside the path leading to the lake, he is bent over a snapping turtle the size of a Thanksgiving turkey. Louise doesn't know which to look at first, the long brown back of the boy or the spiky ridged shell of the turtle. So she stands there in the middle of the road looking from one to the other. Then the boy straightens up and turns toward Louise. "Oh my God," is what she says. She hopes he will think she is talking about the turtle.

"Ever see one this big?" he asks, nudging the shell with the toe of one work-booted foot and hitching his belt slightly so the hammer hangs down his left hip. His upper body is bare, his shoulders smooth and deeply muscled. His eyes and hair are almost black, and he has a red bandanna tied around his head. He is smiling at her.

"Not for a long time." Louise notices the turtle's head come poking out of its shell. "Careful," she warns him, "he might bite you." She is a mother, first and foremost.

"Nah, he wouldn't dare. I'm so mean I have to sleep with one eye open so I don't kick myself in the ass." He laughs, seeming to find himself vastly entertaining. His teeth are remarkably white, and there is a fine powdering of sawdust on his right cheekbone that she would like to brush off. "Don't you come too close, is all," he says to her. "This baby take you in his mouth, no telling when he'd turn you loose." He grins at Louise, who is oddly flustered. She feels fourteen years old. The boy shows no sign of boredom, of turning away from her, no sign of having anything better to do than to stand there and talk to her. She looks around to see who it is he is really talking to. Some young girl somewhere he is trying to impress.

"You up here for the whole summer?" he is asking her now. She shakes her head. "Friend of Mrs. Townshend's?" She nods. "Nice lady," the boy says, "very nice lady." He pauses. "So how long are you staying?"

"Just a week," she says. "I'm from New York."

"Figured that," he says, pulling a crumpled pack of Marlboros out of the back pocket of his jeans. "Smoke?" He offers her one.

"No, I quit. Three packs a day I used to do." Louise is bragging. She watches him cup his hands around the cigarette he is lighting, shake out the match and flick it in the dirt.

"No, I mean do you *smoke*," he says, making the quick sucking sounds of a joint.

"Oh, do I smoke. No," she says firmly, "I hate to smoke. I get paranoid."

He cocks his head to one side. "No kidding?" he says. "Not me. Hey, know what I call paranoia? Heightened awareness," and he cracks himself up again. He takes another drag and says after a moment's hesitation, "Would you like to see the countryside around here? I can take you for a drive later. That's my truck," he says proudly, pointing to a black Ford pickup parked a little down the road. It has a bumper sticker that reads TOO CUTE TO STAY HOME.

In one of those moments Louise is famous for, when she decides to do something without thinking, she says, "Yes, sure. Thank you very much." And then regrets it. "Well," she says, "see you," and hurries into her cabin where she goes directly to the bathroom and peers at herself in the mirror.

"Who was he talking to?" she asks out loud.

"SO WHEN is he picking you up?" Mona asks. The twins are having lunch in their highchairs.

"I don't know," says Louise. "I ran away. I'm not going."

"Of course you're going," says Mona, cutting up a hot dog for the twins. "You're doing it for me," she says. "If you don't, we'll both get old. Now go sit out there on that porch and wait for him to tell you what time."

"I can't. I feel like an enormous piece of bait," says Louise. "I feel like a ridiculous elderly baby bird."

"Out," says Mona firmly. "I'm going to ask Bridget to clean in here, and you have to be outside in the sun," she says, spooning mashed potato into Ernie's little mouth.

LOUISE SITS tilted back in her chair. She has Auden face down in her lap, her own face turned toward the sun. Her legs and feet are bare against the railing of the deck. The house is built on a wooded hill above a lake, and through the trees Louise can see water glittering in the sun. She has been remembering the first time a boy opened her clothes. It was 1957 or '58, she and Tommy Morell were leaning against the scaffolding of what was to become the Loeb Student Center in Washington Square. She was wearing a new blue coat from the now-long-defunct De Pinna, it was freezing cold and they were standing out of the wind, kissing. She can remember today the taste of his mouth: decay and wintergreens. Every time somebody walked past, she would hide her face against his shoulder. And then she felt his hands on the front of her coat, the sensation taking a moment to travel through the many layers of her clothes, like light from a star; and his fingers were working at the buttons, the many small difficult buttons of this coat, and she was not pushing his hands away. Louise sighs. Amazing what else she has forgotten, but this scrap of memory is as real as yesterday. This morning.

Louise is deep in daydream when hammering begins under the porch, startling her. Sitting in her thin cotton dress, the hammering directly beneath feels particularly intimate. She hears murmuring of men's voices, and the next thing she knows the boy has swung himself up over the railing, defying God knows what laws of physics, and is hunkering down next to her on the porch.

"So I'll pick you up at seven-thirty? I need to go home and get a shower first. Okay?"

"Well, sure," she says, "that's fine. Sure."

"See you later," and he grins and bounds back off the deck. His head reappears a moment later. "I'm Donny," he says. "You're—?"

"Louise."

"Just wear what you have on," advises Mona, after Louise has changed her clothes three times. "That nice dress that buttons down the front."

"You don't think I look as if I'm trying to look like Little Bo-Peep?"

"Louise, that's the last thing I'd say you looked like. You look fine. You look really good, in fact. No wonder he asked you."

"Mona, what are we going to talk about? What am I going to say to this boy? I'm forty-fucking-six years old. I certainly can't talk about my kids. They're probably older than he is."

"I don't think you're going to be doing a whole lot of talking," says Mona. "I don't think talk is Donny's specialty."

Donny comes to the door to pick her up just like a real

date. He is wearing a shirt tonight, which has the odd effect of making him seem even younger. Louise feels awkward when he says hello to Mona, calls Tony "sir." Louise can't get out of there fast enough. "Take my sweater, Louise," calls Mona. "It's outside there on the rocker."

Donny opens the door of the truck and closes it behind her when she is safely inside. Then he runs around and hops up on the driver's side. "Do you have any idea how old I am?" asks Louise when they are both sitting in the truck. She feels she should get this over with right away.

"Well, I know you're older than me," Donny turns to look at her. "I figure you're twenty-eight or so." Twenty-eight or so? Dear God. Twenty-eight or so?

"Oh," says Louise, "how old are you?"

"I'll be twenty-one next month."

"You're twenty," says Louise, closing her eyes briefly. "You're twenty years old."

"Yeah, but I'll be twenty-one next month," he repeats, and turns the key in the ignition and the truck starts to vibrate pleasantly, reminding Louise, not surprisingly, of an enormously powerful animal just barely held in check. "Ready?" he asks.

She is looking at how loosely his hand rests on the stick

shift. She nods, watching his hand tighten on the stick, the muscles in his arm bulging slightly as he puts the truck in first and they begin lurching down the steep path that leads to the highway.

"Wahoo!" he yells, thrusting his body half out the window, then he ducks back in and grins at Louise. "Couldn't help it," he says sheepishly. "I just feel good." She smiles at him.

Louise is now completely at ease. As soon as the truck started moving she felt something inside her click into place. She knows exactly who she is and what she is doing. She is a blond-headed woman in the front seat of a moving vehicle, she is nobody's mother, nobody's former wife, nobody's anything. Louise is a girl again.

A mile down the highway Donny fishes around under his seat and comes up with a Sucrets box, which he hands her. "Can you light me up the joint? Matches on the dash." Louise opens the box and picks the joint up. It is lying next to loose grass and on top of a bunch of rolling papers. Louise hasn't smoked a joint in a long time. The last time she did, she became convinced that she was about to become dinner: about to be minced, put in a cream sauce, and run under the broiler. She was at a party being given by her then-new husband's old friends.

"I don't really smoke," she begins, and then, "Oh, what the hell," she says, shrugging, and lights the joint. "Maybe I've changed," she says, talking mostly to herself.

"Maybe the company has changed," says Donny, and she can't imagine what he thinks he means by that, but they are passing the joint back and forth, and Louise is beginning to feel pretty good. Something lovely is happening deep in her throat, some awareness she has never experienced before. "God, I've got such an interesting *throat*," she says, and Donny laughs.

"You're getting high," he says.

"I am?" Louise sits up straight.

"You okay? Feeling okay?"

"I think I feel good," she says, taking stock. "Yes," she announces rather formally, "I feel really quite good." Donny slows down and takes a right turn into what he calls a sand pit. It is a parking area off the road, behind a kind of berm. "Let's roll another," he says, proceeding to do so. Louise watches fascinated; she has always loved watching people use their hands. When he licks the paper to seal the cigarette she sees his tongue is pink.

This kid's tongue is actually pink, oh lordy lordy, thinks Louise.

"Why don't you have a girlfriend?" she wants to know.

"I had a girlfriend. She moved out three months ago. She left me a note saying she was going to Wyoming." Donny snaps the Sucrets box shut now and looks for the matches.

"Oh. Crummy. Were you sad?"

"For a while. Thing that made it easier was she took my damn stereo. Hard to be sad and pissed at the same time. But yeah, we had some good times. Bummed me out she couldn't tell me to my face she was going."

"She probably wouldn't have been able to leave, then."

"Yeah. That's what she said in her note." He offers her the new joint to light, but she shakes her head.

"What was her name?"

"Robin. But anybody asks me now 'how's Robin?' know what I say? 'Robin who?' I say, 'Robin who?'" Donny laughs and then turns his head to look out the window. "Company," he says, as a red Toyota pulls in. "Let's go somewhere a little less public. Want to see the lake?"

"Sure," says Louise. "Anything." What a nice state Maine is to provide sand pits and lakes for its citizens to park in, Louise is thinking. They head off and stop along the way to see the school Donny was kicked out of. It is a plain, one-story brick building that Louise thinks privately looks pretty depressing, but Donny is driving around it slowly, almost lovingly. "You had a good time here?" she asks him.

"Yep. I had a good time here."

"How come they kicked you out?"

"Oh, this and that. I was a hothead then, I guess. I'm a lot calmer now, though you might not believe it. Straightening myself out. Full-time job in itself," he laughs. "Full-time job in itself."

"I like hotheaded," says Louise. "I always did."

Donny, who has been circling the school building, pulls over to the far end of the lot and parks under a tree. Turns the engine off and they look at each other in the fading light of the summer evening, a little moon starting to show between the trees; a street light blinks on thirty feet away. They look at each other, and then he reaches quite frankly for her, or perhaps she reaches for him, but his hands are on her dress, the front of her dress at the buttons, and his dark head is against her neck, his breath everywhere. Her hands are in his hair, under his shirt, feeling the tight muscles of his belly above his belt. Fumbling. Then they are kissing, and, because his window does not close completely, the truck fills with mosquitoes, and they are kissing and slapping and slapping and cursing and laughing and kissing and kissing and kissing. Donny drags a blanket out from behind his seat, and they stumble out of the truck and onto the grass, and Louise is lying down under a million or so stars. "I wanted to fuck you the first time I saw you, to tell you the truth," Donny is whispering as he lowers his body down on hers.

They sleep in the truck that night, parked near the lake that seems to be everywhere. Or rather, Donny sleeps, his head in Louise's lap. Louise is awake all night, watching the woods drain of moonlight and fill up again slowly with a misty brightness that seems to rise from the ground. Donny's body is arranged somehow around the gearshift, his head and shoulders resting on Louise. He sleeps like a baby. She looks at his closed eyes, dark lashes, his straight black brows. His skin is beautiful, like silk. Dear God, how came this beautiful wild child to be asleep in my lap, thinks Louise. At six, she jiggles his shoulder. "Time to wake up," she says. "We've been gone all night."

"What if I refuse to take you back?" he asks sleepily. "Suppose I just decide to keep you?"

MONA IS up, of course, when Louise gets in. The twins are out with Bridget; little Joe and Tony are down by the lake doing something with boats. "Don't let Tony see you," says Mona. "I told him you got in late last night. You know Tony." Tony has never approved of Louise, not since she asked him if she could upend herself in his laundry hamper. "For the pheromones," she had explained. "It's been so long since the last good kiss." Louise had read somewhere that women who lived without the company of men were apt to age more quickly.

"Why can't she just ride the subway at rush hour?" Tony had asked irritably. "Plenty of nice hair tonic and body sweat in there. Why does it have to be my laundry?"

"So?" says Mona now, pouring two cups of coffee. "Or don't I really want to know?"

"I'll say one word," says Louise, "to satisfy your curiosity, because I know it's on your mind. Hung."

"*Comme* zee horse?" Mona is leaning forward.

"*Comme* zee horse."

"Ahhhh."

"And you know what else? I like him, I actually like him. He's working so hard to grow up. His girlfriend left him, and he had to move back with his parents because he couldn't afford the rent by himself. He works his ass off. I like him."

"Yeah? Well, great, but don't start taking this seriously."

"He's picking me up again tonight. You know what? Staying up all night makes me feel young again, isn't that weird? I haven't been this tired since I was young."

"Go lie down. I'll wake you up at lunch."

"Mona? I loved not talking about my kids. It was like being twenty myself, you know? It was like not having a tail I had to fit everywhere. I'm never going to tell anyone about my kids again."

"Louise, you're delirious. Go upstairs and lie down."

"Good night."

"Louise?" calls Mona, as Louise disappears up the stairs. "You're being careful? I'm not talking about babies, you know what I'm talking about."

Louise's head appears around the corner. "Mona," she says, "Do you think I was born yesterday?"

Two days later Donny takes off work. "I've got vacation

time coming," he says. "I'm taking you four-wheeling. That is if you want to drive around with me for a few days."

Mona is worried. "I hope you're not taking this seriously," she keeps saying. "I know how you can get, Louise, and I don't want you to get involved with a twenty-year-old boy who lives with his parents."

"Come on, Mona, I haven't had this much fun in my whole life," says Louise. "I'm twenty years old myself this week. The last time I was twenty I had two children and an ex-husband in the making."

Mona's expression relaxes. "All right, but I don't want to hear a word of complaint out of you for eighteen months, and I hope you have plenty of raw meat for the trip."

LOUISE FEELS like a summer house this kid has broken into, pushing his way through doors that haven't been opened in years, snapping up blinds, windows, pulling dust covers off furniture, shaking rugs, curtains, bouncing on the beds. A fine, honorable old house, and he appreciates the way it has been made, the way it has lasted, the strength of its structure, noble old dimensions. It has been a long time since Louise was put to such good use.

"What's the longest you've ever gone without making love?" she asks him.

"Fifteen years," he answers.

Louise loves his raw energy, and the lavish way he squanders it on pointless undertakings, impossible feats, such as driving the truck directly up the steep woodside of a mountain whenever he thinks he spies faint tracks. (Louise sees only dense woods.) He screeches the truck to a stop, leaps down to lock the front wheels, jumps back inside to do something sexy to the gears, pausing to kiss Louise for five minutes, and then he coaxes, bullies, cajoles the truck off the road and into the trees. Louise loves it. She loves everything about him by now. She loves the muscles in his shoulders, the veins in his forearms. "I like how you touch me," he whispers. She wants him to explain everything he knows, the difference between a dug and an artesian well, how to build a ladder, hang a door, put a roof on. "You're really interested?" he asks her. "You really want to know?" She nods. "The plumb line is God," he begins gravely.

Louise is as close to carefree as she has ever been. There is nothing behind her, her past is not part of this trip, and nothing in front but a dashboard full of music and the open road. They like the same music, sing the same songs. Stevie Ray Vaughn, the Georgia Satellites, Tom Petty and the Heartbreakers. "Break Down" is their favorite song and they blast it all week, yelling it out the windows, singing it to each other in the truck, and then they collapse laughing, this forty-six-year-old woman and this twenty-year-old boy, who are having the time of their lives. They rent a room in a motel when they get tired of fighting off the mosquitoes. Louise uses her Visa card expecting any minute the long arm of the law to grab her by the collar, bring her to her senses. Donny is bent over the register saying, "You'll want an address?" and Louise hears the manager saying, "Oh, just put anything," with a knowing snicker. For just a second, she feels gawky, naked. How many good years does she have left, she wonders, before she appears pathetic. Right now she can still get away with it, but fifty approaches, the hill she will one day be over is looming in the distance. So when the manager shows them the room and it contains two double-decker beds, one cot, and a king-size four-poster, Louise rubs her hands together largely for his benefit and says, "Good. We can really use the room."

They order Chinese take-out that night from an improbable place down the road, and Louise bites down into something hard in her moo shu pork and, spitting it into her hand, she sees it is a human tooth. She hurries into the bathroom and locks the door. "You all right in there?" asks Donny, knocking. It is Louise's tooth, her temporary cap, and she rinses it off and jams it back in her mouth praying to God it will stay. "Donny," she says, coming out of the bathroom. "I've got to tell you how old I am. Guess what, I'm forty-six." He doesn't seem particularly interested. "I'm forty-six, did you hear me?"

"Yeah?" He is lying down on the big bed, his hands behind his head. "So?"

"And what's more I have four kids, and three of them are older than you, and I have two grandchildren on top of that." Louise seems out of breath all of a sudden. He just looks at her.

"Come here," he says. She goes there. He grabs her hand. "I guess that makes me some kind of motherfucker," he says with a lazy grin, pulling her down on the bed. "Stick with me, I won't let you get old," he says, into her hair. "But I am old," she wants to moan, "I already am old."

"Why are a woman's breasts always softest in the evening?" he wants to know, pulling her toward him.

Louise is awake all night. "You can't kiss all the time," a friend of hers once said, by way of explaining having picked up a few words of Italian one summer. "You can't kiss all the time." Louise thinks she knows this, she knows it is time to go back to the grown-ups, back to New York, her office. Back to real life. This isn't real life, this relationship relies too heavily on rock 'n' roll and the open road. Real life is not this dream come true, it is long winter nights with nothing to talk about. You can't kiss all the time. "I'll build you a house," Donny said yesterday. "Stay. I'll build you a house."

He knows before she tells him that she is going home. He is quiet all morning, sullen even. "What's the matter?" she asks, but he shakes off her hand.

"You're leaving."

"But I'm coming back. I'm coming back for your birthday."

"But you're leaving, right?"

She nods.

"Well, I'm bummed."

She tells him about the office, the mail, her apartment,

bills unpaid, her daughter coming home from Europe soon.

"What do you want for your birthday?" she asks him.

"You."

"You've got me. What else?"

"More of you."

"You've got me. What else?"

"Am I asking too much?"

BACK IN New York, Louise is lonelier than she expected to be. New York is gritty, dirty, sad. Her apartment is so empty, quiet. Louise is of an age now when most of the men in her life are former lovers who fly in from nowhere for a couple of days every six years or so; they sit on her chairs, eat at her table, sleep in her bed, and when they leave they leave a kind of half-life behind, an absence so palpable it is almost a presence. The furniture rebukes Louise on these occasions. "So where'd he go?" asks the white sofa, the pink chair. The bed. But Donny has never been here, so she has to conjure up his memory out of whole cloth, so to speak. And she misses him more than she thought she would.

In fact, she talks of little else. She is as apt to pull pictures of Donny out of her wallet as of her grandsons. "You're in luck," she might have said a month ago, "I have fifty-three new pictures of my grandsons." Now she takes seven photographs out of her wallet, they are all of Donny, and she lays them out on the table like a row of solitaire. "So," she says, to anyone who will listen. "You know that poem by Auden? 'Lay your sleeping head my love'?" Her friends are respectful, for the most part silent. They let her play it out.

"Do we sleep with the young to stay young ourselves or just to lie down next to all that beauty?" Louise wants to know. Mona is irritated. They are together in Riverside Park with the kids. Joe is in the sandbox, Mona and Louise are pushing the twins in the little swings. "Neither," says Mona. "How should I know?" she snaps. Then, more gently, "To lie down next to all that beauty."

"I knew it," says Louise, hopping. "I knew it!"

"I'm worried about you," says Mona. "I mean, I hope you're not being faithful to him or anything."

Louise bursts out laughing. "Come on, Mona. Who am I going to go out with? The dry cleaner?"

"I'm just concerned you might get hurt. You let your emotions get involved."

"Well, of course I let my emotions get involved. What the hell is the point if you don't let your emotions get involved? But it's not like going out for ice cream and coming home and saying, 'Gee, I wish I hadn't had that ice cream.' I liked the kid. I loved the kid, if you want to know."

"Just what I was afraid of. And I certainly don't think you should go back up there for his birthday. Enough is enough."

"I promised him I'd go. I promised him."

BUT LOUISE has not heard from Donny, and though she has left messages with his mother (an exquisitely humiliating experience), he has not returned her calls. The night before she is supposed to get on the bus she finally gets him on the phone. She does not want to keep her end of the bargain and wind up sitting on a suitcase in a parking lot in Portland waiting for Godot. It is a bad connection, and she can barely hear him, and she has to keep repeating "What?" into the telephone like an old woman with an ear trumpet.

"Are we still on for tomorrow?" she shouts, although she already knows the answer.

"Things have changed around here," Donny says. His voice sounds so foreign, so young.

"So do you still want me to come up tomorrow?" Louise is amazed at how painful this is.

"I guess now is not a good time," he says, but she can barely hear him.

"What?"

"No," he says, "not this time."

"Well, Happy Birthday to you," she says, hanging up the phone.

"WOULD YOU mind removing your lipstick?" asks Dr. Chan, handing Louise a tissue. He always makes this request, but Louise wears it to his office just the same. She likes to look her best for the dentist. Dr. Chan wears his hair cut short except for three very long, very skinny braids, and Louise has always been too shy to inquire as to their significance.

"Today we put in your permanent tooth," says Dr. Chan, setting out his instruments, mixing his little pots of cement.

"That's good," says Louise, "because this one fell out over the summer and I had to put it back myself. 'A tooth for every child,'" she adds, but Dr. Chan does not ask after her meaning.

She settles back in her chair. The land of menopause stretches out behind her closed lids, as Dr. Chan easily removes the temporary cap. It seems to be a quiet place, resembling a kind of savannah. There are mountains in the distance. There doesn't appear to be much activity beyond a certain amount of flank-nuzzling, as far as Louise can tell. But who knows? She has heard some odd cries at night, down by the water hole.

LOVE IN THE PRESENT TENSE

Louise is outside the Cathedral Market staring at oranges when who should show up but Henry Gold, former love of her life. "You," she says, her heart jumping. Henry reaches out to touch the collar of her coat, and they stand joined like that a moment among the heaps of fruit and the flowers and the boxes of vegetables.

"I was in the neighborhood," says Henry. "How about a cup of coffee?"

"Goddamn it, Henry," says Louise. It has been years since they died from love. "You're supposed to be gone."

"Just a cup of coffee," says Henry, his eyes the color of bare hills. "I have so much to tell you."

"What?" says Louise, turning to jerk a plastic bag from the roll above her head. "You have what to tell me?"

179

"Everything. I don't know. I miss you. I wrote fifty poems. I met a dancer."

"I love knowing that."

"I haven't slept with anyone else."

"Good for you." Louise is busy with oranges.

"And if I had, I would have been thinking of you."

"Oh, Henry," says Louise. "Shut up." But she turns and smiles, and he takes hold of her sleeve, still careful not to touch Louise herself. Henry has a deep respect for outer garments and for allowing the inevitable its moment of delicacy. "All right," says Louise. "One cup of coffee."

Henry drops three plums into her basket. They have been up his sleeve the whole time, and they roll off his palm one by one. "Magic," says Henry. He is wearing an old overcoat from the Salvation Army in Easton, Pennsylvania. It cost five bucks ten years ago, Louise remembers. Henry is not interested so much in the bargain, he wants ghosts in his clothes. He likes wondering what another man kept in those deep pockets. He writes poems about it.

"She never heard of the St. Valentine's Day Massacre," he tells Louise as they walk up Broadway with their bags of fruit.

"Who?"

"The dancer. We were in an underground garage and I told her what it reminded me of, and she'd never heard of it."

"No kidding," says Louise, trying to remember it herself.

"How can you hold a woman in your arms who never heard of the St. Valentine's Day Massacre? How can you take her seriously?" Henry gestures in the air with his little bag of plums.

"Why are you telling me this?" says Louise, stopping dead in her tracks. "Jesus Christ!"

Henry shoots her that look of faded love, familiar as old clothes, love that has been out in the elements for years, rained on, sunned on, stonewashed. Louise is a sucker for this particular look.

"Damn it," she says, but she is smiling.

"I'm in this for the pleasure," she told him years ago, rather naively, as things turned out. "I'm in it for the pain," Henry had said with a grin. They were drinking coffee in the Danté Cafe, Henry was doodling her name on the napkins. She was wearing the blue dress. They had known each other for three days.

Henry is back in her kitchen, and Louise is precariously happy. He sets the fruit in a bowl and she fusses at the stove. She does not know yet whether this will be leave-taking or renewal, with Henry it is always a little of both. "I've been working on a poem," she tells him, shyly. Henry is a poet, Louise writes poems. She thinks he might like this one, the lines are longer, it has a fern in it and much darkness. "You are a complicated woman with complicated emotions," Henry had told her once. "You should be writing serious poems."

Henry takes the poem to the kitchen table, then rises to read the last lines out loud.

"'Love, you old eyesore / Your sleeve in the soup / Get out of my life.'" Henry nods his approval. "I like it," he says, his fingers at the buttons of her dress. "This is a serious poem."

"It is," says Louise, batting down his hand.

The day, which began as spring, has turned sharply colder. Snow is in the forecast. Henry's little orange car will never make it back to Pennsylvania. Henry will be spending the night.

"I don't think we should make love," he says. They are standing on either side of the bed.

"Me neither," says Louise, who had been thinking the opposite.

"It would be too upsetting," says Henry, taking off his watch, placing it carefully on the night table.

"You bet," says Louise, from somewhere inside her dress.

"For both of us," Henry continues, unbuttoning his shirt.

"For both of us," says Louise, pulling the last of her clothes over her head and tossing them toward the chair. She slips into bed. "Good night," she says.

"I take it back," says Henry, a moment or two later. She can feel his warm breath.

"I don't," she says recklessly, shrugging him off. Then she lies awake, listening to his breathing. "What are you doing here?" she finally whispers, but he is asleep and she is stranded like a shell left by the tide. She turns on her side, looking at the curtains, at the lights moving on the wall, at the flowers Henry bought on the street. They lean against the rim of the glass, reminding her of the Chinese woman she once saw who in one incongruously graceful motion stretched far out over the curb to spit.

In the middle of the night Louise wakes up. The light is

on in the kitchen. Henry is sitting at the red table, a glass of tea at his elbow. He is writing.

"You okay?" she asks, tying her bathrobe. It is snowing now. The city sky looks curiously pink with the storm.

"No," says Henry. He looks sad and weary. "Was I wrong to come?"

"Oh Christ, Henry, I don't know. I'm sad with you and I'm sad without you." She is standing behind his chair, her hands on his shoulders.

"Sit with me a while," says Henry.

"It's three in the morning."

"Tomorrow is Sunday, you don't have to get up. Sit with me." So she sits down. He is writing a play, he tells her, a play in verse. One of the characters is a blue dress, her blue dress, the one he loved her in, the one he liked pretending had a soul. He wants to question the dress, writing down its answers for his play. Louise must be its voice, this is partly why he has come, he tells her now.

"I don't want to do this. I can't do this."

"Just say whatever comes into your head."

"Nothing will come into my head."

"Please. It will be easy. Just try."

"All right," says Louise unhappily. "Wait. I'll get it."

She goes to find the dress, which is hanging on the back of the closet door. She sits down, holding the small blue bundle in her lap.

Henry is ready, his pencil poised.

"When did you stop loving me?" The poet asks the dress.

"Never," it answers with her voice.

"Henry," says Louise, standing up. "I can't do this."

"Just one more question," he asks.

"Make it up," says Louise, disappearing down the hall.

THE NEXT morning Louise is measuring beans for coffee when Henry announces he will be leaving by noon. It seems he really has met a dancer although it is nothing serious, he assures her. "I didn't know you were invited to stick around that long," says Louise lightly.

Henry is in a marvelous mood. He is describing the Turner show to Louise, most particularly some pigeons painted on a roof. From a distance of six feet they are unmistakably pigeons on a roof, but viewed up close they are just two little dabs of paint. How does he do it! Henry wants to know. Just two little dabs of paint!

"He has them stored up inside his shoulder like eggs in a chicken," Louise tells him. "And they travel down his arm and out the end of the paintbrush. He was born with a certain number of them up there."

Henry looks at her. "You are right," he says. "I love you. Do you know that?"

"I love you, too," says Louise. "So what?"

Henry says things that would look silly in print. "I am not afraid to die when I'm with you," he told her once. Louise is younger than Henry, death is not much on her mind. Or rather, she dies all the time, but nothing comes of it.

"I showed the dancer my poems," Henry tells her later.

"I don't want to hear about your dancer."

"No, listen, I want to tell you. Do you know what she said?"

"I don't care what she said."

"She said, 'What is a pickerel?'"

"Do you have pickerels in it?"

"But that was all she said! She asked me what a pickerel was. 'A fish!' I said. 'It's a fish!'" Henry is cackling like a madman.

"Henry," says Louise, "maybe you've finally met your match."

"Do you think so?" asks Henry quickly, touching her

hand. "Will you go to Quebec with me next spring?" Henry is leaving a line in the water.

"No," says Louise, to her own surprise.

"Ireland?"

"No, Henry." She is helping him into his coat, his back is to her.

"Turkey? Greece? The Isle of Wight?" They are standing in the little hall beside the door. "I miss you," he says, turning around, and his voice is soft and low and full of places to lie down. Once upon a time Louise could stretch out full length in Henry Gold's voice.

"I miss you, too," she says, matter-of-factly. "I miss you all the time."

"Is this it?" Henry does not ask. He just stands there with his arms around her.

"This is it, Henry," she does not say, "this is all she wrote."

Later, Louise imagines something. She will put on the blue dress. She will come up behind Henry while he is still staring out the window. She will turn him around to face her, and his hands will tremble as he undoes the buttons, as if afraid to tear the woman's skin inside, as if she might be made of tissue paper, or of flowers.

GETTING OVER TOM

Shortly after Louise's fortieth birthday—

"What?"

Shortly after Louise's fortieth birthday—

"Why do you always put in her age?" Louise sits up. She has been lolling on the couch. I am hard at work at the desk.

One night when Louise was bowling—

"Why are you starting there? I never bowl." Louise has gotten up and is now breathing down my neck.

"Look," I say. "Do you want to write this yourself?"

"No, no, I don't. Sorry. Actually, I was forty-four." She sounds penitent. She goes back to lie down on the couch.

Louise was forty-four, and Tom was thirty-nine—

"I thought you were writing about Dick?"

"I think this is more about Tom, don't you? *Getting*

189

Over Tom I thought I'd call it." I am trying to be patient.

"But you've got no ending for that, that just trailed off."

"I'm going to bring Dick in at the end. He was part of getting over Tom, wasn't he?"

"Not really. He was an act of generosity. Make sure you put in about the goodness of my heart and everything. Make sure I appear vulnerable and not too shallow."

"I don't think this is shallow at all, Louise. I think it is very depressing."

"Okay. Start. I'll be quiet unless you leave something out."

"EVERYBODY WANTS to be held," said Tom, the littlest Texan. Louise had met him at a bowling alley, kissed him near the Coke machine. "Where did you learn to kiss like that—" Louise gasped, "so lightly?"

"Actually, it was Tom who said that," Louise interrupts.

"Look, Louise," I say. "Do you want to appear sympathetic or what?"

"Of course I do."

"Then let her say it. It will make you look better."

"This is getting awfully complicated."

"I'm starting again," I say.

"EVERYBODY WANTS to be held," said Tom, the littlest Texan. Louise had met him at the bowling alley, kissed him by the Coke machine. Where did you learn to kiss like that—" Louise gasped, "so lightly?"

"I've got a ride home," she said moments later to Helen. "Don't wait up."

Louise and Tom repaired to his truck, a Silverado, where they made love on the front seat.

"Not exactly love," Louise interrupts again.

And then they drove to his apartment in nearby Goshen.

"Did you notice how my game fell off after we kissed?" Tom asked Louise several hours later, winning her heart with those words.

"Precisely," says Louise to me. "Isn't it funny how the heart works?"

Everything was wrong with Tom. He was short, he subscribed to Reader's Digest, *he looked forward every week to watching "Lifestyles of the Rich and Famous," and he had voted twice for Ronnie.*

But everybody wants to be held.

"He did say that," Louise can't help repeating, breaking my train of thought again. "That's another reason I liked him so much. He said, 'Everybody wants to be held,' in a very nice voice."

Tom was a very nice man, and despite the difference in their backgrounds Louise began entertaining thoughts of marriage. He took her fishing one weekend, and they talked of Niagara Falls. Not for a honeymoon, just for the sights. Tom knew a way to get behind the water.

"All men have a specialty," Tom said to Louise one morning as they lay in bed discussing life. "Mine is locating leaks."

Louise liked imagining him with his face pressed against the damp white plaster walls, like a doctor, a woman wailing in the background, "Where is it coming from?"

"You just hold tight, little lady," Tom might say. "I'll have this solved in a jiffy."

"You're having too good a time," Louise says to me. "Whenever you laugh like that when you're writing I know it's time to worry."

"Trust me, Louise," I say, "just for once. If I think it's funny, maybe somebody else will think it's funny, too."

"But suppose they think it's arch? Just think of that for one minute, will you?"

"There are worse things than arch. There's cranky humorlessness."

"I'm not sure that's worse, really, please think about this. This is not the final draft, is it?"

"God, no. Why don't you take a little nap?"

Louise lies back down on the couch, puts the pillow over her head. "I think I need a blanket," she says, getting up once more. She pokes around in the hall closet. "God. I've got to clean this out," she says.

"But not now," I say, getting angry at last. "Shut up. Just shut the fuck up."

Tom, the littlest Texan, was actually in love with a florist in Dallas, Texas, his hometown. But the florist was a married woman. One night a stranger had come up to Tom and laid a slug on the bar in front of him. "This one I'm showing you," the stranger said. "The next one you won't see."

"I can take a hint," Tom told Louise. "I left that night. I'll be up here until the whole thing blows over."

Tom liked making breakfast. "Huevos rancheros," he said, "you make them with love," and he grinned at Louise, shaking the tabasco sauce.

"Are you going to tell about how Louise felt when she

answered his door that morning?" Louise is on her elbow again, giving me her two cents' worth.

"You mean when the kids were there?"

"Uh huh."

"Do you think that's important?" I ask her.

"Well, yes, it was kind of an epiphany, wasn't it? I mean Tom was in the shower, and Louise answered the door in his bathrobe, and two little children were standing there and their little mouths dropped open. And Louise thought, Good Lord, I will figure in their lives forever as the traumatic moment when they saw living proof that their good buddy Tom, who liked to play with dogs, had a sex life. And she felt so surreal, her maternal instinct was nowhere in reach. She just sort of stood there like a fact. They have a mother at home, thought Louise to herself. Let her explain this."

"Can you think of a way to say that sort of sympathetically? So she doesn't seem too much of a hussy?"

"Didn't I just do that?"

I shake my head.

"Well, do you want to put in about her own kids? That her usual response to most situations is to try and make everything okay for everybody? But suddenly she didn't feel responsible or guilty that two little kids had to factor in her existence in their neighbor's life."

"Did you actually say 'factor in' just now?"

"I did and I'm sorry. I'll leave the rest of this up to you. In your capable hands, so to speak." Louise lies back down, throws only one final shot at me. "Don't you wish you had a cigarette?"

Not a month after Louise had seen the last of Tom, who had returned to Texas, a man appeared at Louise's office door. He had something for the gallery, he told her. Could he leave it with Louise? He was big and shivering and his eyes were too close together. He was wearing a red flannel shirt and a pair of jeans, and outside it was howling rain.

"He wasn't unattractive," says Louise, raising her head. "He just wasn't my type."

"I don't believe you have a type," I say, a trifle acidly.

He was big and rawboned, and he had a parcel of drawings.

"They were good," says Louise, sitting up again. "He had one of a kitchen windowsill with all this stuff on it." She lies back dreamily. "He really was a very good artist. He just talked too much. Dick Something Something the Third. A trust fund boy, but he had talent."

Dick was a talker. Once inside the door he began talking and it was like chain-smoking, the end of one story lit up the start of the next. He drowned his own self out. Everything he said came out sounding the same, like different lengths of toothpaste. Louise found herself pitying him.

"It's not that he was boring," Louise rouses herself to tell me, "although he was. It was just that he couldn't stop. He told me how his brothers had always teased him and how he was closer to his mother than his father, and his father had always wanted him to be a lawyer, that kind of thing. You know."

He looked to Louise like a stray. They went outside, and he stood there a moment looking forlorn. Louise took advantage of this lull in his conversation. "Where are you going now?" she asked. Well, he didn't exactly know. He had given the key to his apartment to somebody, and he wasn't living in the city right now, and he had not been able to reach his friend. Blah blah blah. It was a complicated story, but the upshot was that he had nowhere to go and he didn't even have an umbrella.

"'Lonely and afraid in a world he never made,' is what Louise said," says Louise.

Louise looked at her watch. "Look," she said, "I'm freez-

ing to death. If you want to come home with me I'll cook us some supper and you can try and call your friend from there."

"Actually," says Louise, "I wasn't cold a bit. I had on my hat with the three roses on it and my big purple coat I got last year on sale, and I was wearing my boots. I just didn't want him to think I thought he was a wuss for shivering. You know how sensitive men can be."

The first thing he did when they got to Louise's apartment was fish something out of Louise's sink.

"No, it wasn't. The first thing he did was tell me about his wife. Her name was Portia, and for fifteen minutes it was Portia this and Portia that, like a spell to keep him safe. 'Weave a something round him thrice,' whatever. As if he thought I was going to jump his bones. Then he looked in the sink."

Soon after arriving at Louise's apartment, Dick fished something out of her sink. "Shouldn't this be on a shelf somewhere?" he asked. The fact is Louise kept a small pre-Columbian head in her sink because it seemed the best place for it while she made up her mind whether she wanted to keep it or throw it away. It was small, not much bigger than a pecan, and she could never remember where she'd gotten it, only that it always wound up in the kitchen sink. "Oh dear," she said, and put it in her apron pocket next to the wadded-up napkin and the two pens and the apple stem with three leaves still attached. Then she put it back in the sink.

Dick told her all about the museum in Mexico City, and she listened politely although she had been there herself.

She made him supper—

"Cut to the chase," says Louise. "This is getting very boring."

I glare at her. "It's your life," I want to say, "you have no one to blame but yourself," but I hold my tongue.

By midnight Louise knew all about Dick Something Something the Third. She had been a good listener. It was raining hard, and Louise yawned. "You can sleep on the couch if you want to," she said, liking the idea of a warm man in her house. Like a fireplace that talked. "I can get you a pillow and some blankets."

When she came back into the living room, he was lying full length on the couch, and he had taken his clothes off down to his underwear. He had on a white undershirt and boxer shorts. Pale blue. His hands were behind his head, and the skin of his arms was so white it fascinated Louise, and the muscles were large and round, they looked like two croquet balls.

"They did. Exactly," says Louise. "God. And the skin was like the underbelly of certain fish, and there were little black hairs, and it was really very interesting."

Louise sat down on the edge of her chair.

"Would you fit here?" Dick asked her, pointing to a narrow strip of couch alongside his body.

"Don't forget he had a wife and I knew it," Louise tells me. "That's important. A nice wife named Portia who picked out his clothes. I wasn't going to lay a glove on him."

"Louise," I say to her. "I would appreciate it if you kept quiet for a moment. You know how hard it is to write these scenes." Louise dives under the pillow and pulls the blanket over her head.

"Tell me when you're done," she says.

"I would just like to hold you, if I may," said Dick to Louise, who was by now in her raggedy nightgown.

"He used those exact words," Louise yells from under the blanket.

Dick put his arms around Louise, and they lay still. Then he sat up abruptly, knocking Louise half to the floor.

"This never works," said Dick, in a very peevish tone, "just holding." And he tore off his undershirt and shorts. Then they—

"He was the kind who arranges your body underneath them," says Louise, interrupting yet again. "You know? Takes one arm and puts it behind your head a little, alters the angle of your head just a fraction of an inch to the left? Like he was getting ready to take a photograph, not fixing to fuck. For these guys you fake it," says Louise. "I faked it for Dick."

"I'm not putting that in," I tell her. "You sound a little too something. Strident, maybe."

"Fuck it," says Louise. "But I didn't get angry until later if you want to be accurate."

In the morning Dick asked Louise a few questions about herself. Louise told him she was getting over a short love affair. She told him about Tom, the littlest Texan. She told him the good things Tom had said, and about the slug on the bar. She told him she had been greatly touched by Tom, how gentle he was, what a good cook. She told him something about Tom had really gotten to her, but she knew it was silly and she would be over it in a month. She told him everybody liked to be held.

Dick looked uncomfortable.

"There I was," says Louise, "grinding beans for his goddamn coffee. I made him the oatmeal that takes forty-five minutes."

Louise put spoons and sugar on the table. She put cream in the pitcher with "Love the Giver" written on it in blue script.

Dick looked uncomfortable and was uncharacteristically silent. Louise thought maybe he was feeling hurt that she had brought up another man. The only sound was the clink of Dick's cereal spoon.

I put the pen down for a minute. "Louise," I say, "I'd feel more comfortable if you could tell me some of the things Dick said. I think a story will be more believable if we show rather than tell, you know what I mean? Give me some of his lengthy dialogue."

"I can't," she says sadly. "I'm sorry. I can't remember much of anything he said. Just a couple of the short things. Can't you make it up? Isn't that what you're partly good for?"

"I can't either," I admit. "I know how to write a boring woman, but I don't seem to be able to write a boring man."

"Oh well," says Louise to me. "Don't let's worry about it yet. You said this isn't the final draft anyway."

Louise took Dick to the subway station. Dick still looked miserable, and he walked like a man with gravel in his shoes. She stood at the entrance to say good-bye. "I probably don't have to say this," Dick began, then stopped, staring at his feet.

"What?" said Louise good-naturedly, as two of her buses went past. "What what what?"

He hemmed and he hawed. Louise glanced at her watch. "Well," said Dick, "you mustn't, you know, talk about me." Louise tried to produce a smile. "What?" she asked.

"Well, you mustn't, please don't tell stories about me. The way you do about Tom. Because I never meant it to happen."

"Wasn't that the limit?" Louise is up from the couch, bounding around the room. "It still makes me mad!"

"Of course I won't," said Louise. "Good-bye and good luck."

Later she kicked the furniture. That night she screeched into the living room air, "What makes you think you're worth a story, you colorless long-winded little shit? Just exactly what kind of story do you think you'd make?"

"THAT IS very satisfying," says Louise to me now. "Thank you very much for writing it down for me."

"You're quite welcome," I say, putting down the pen. "You didn't make it any easier. And I'm a little worried about the head."

"Don't be," says Louise, looking into the sink. "It's still here."

"No, I mean we don't use it as a symbol or anything. We just pick it up and put it back."

"But that's what happened. What's wrong with that?"

"It might be open for interpretation. Maybe they'll come up with something awful."

"Don't worry," says Louise. "What could it possibly mean?" She fills the kettle with water and turns on the heat. "I am very fond of irony," she says, changing the subject. "The older I get the better I like it."

"For my part," I say, "I like a really good cup of coffee."

"Next time," says Louise, putting seven sugars in her cup, "let's call her Cookie and give her really long eyelashes."

"What for?"

"Well, variety. She would have had a completely different life, don't you think? Think how different our lives would have been if we'd been born down South and had names like Cookie or Sugar and had long eyelashes and learned ballroom dancing."

"We went to dancing school," I remind her, "back in 1956. We had to be driven there with whips and chains."

"We were too young," says Louise. "Ballroom dancing is for women past their prime."

"Speak for yourself," I say.

"How reassuring," Louise muses on, paying no attention to me. "How reassuring," she says, closing her eyes, "those little boxes you make with your feet, their hands gently holding yours and the small of your back. They don't love you, but they act as if they do. How preferable to they love you but they act as if they don't."

"That's another story," I say.

"Much too boring," says Louise. Then she gets to her feet and puts on the music. I am already up.

"That's not ballroom," I tell her. "That's Aretha."

"Shut up," says Louise, "and dance."